Ancient Elk Hunt

An Up North Adventure

Ancient Elk Hunt
An Up North Adventure

G.M. Moore

Ancient Elk Hunt
An Up North Adventure

ISBN: 978-1475004625

Printed in the United States of America

For my nephew, Mason, who is the inspiration for Pike, and my nieces, Nicole, Lauren, and Madeline

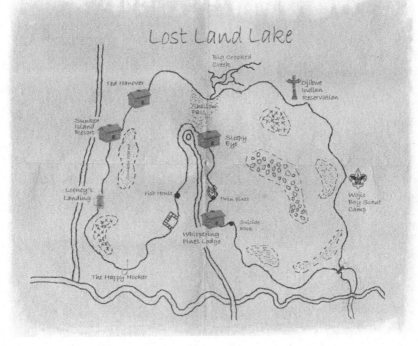

PROLOGUE:
WISCONSIN, BC

A cold wind blew through the dense forest of what would be known ten thousand years later as northern Wisconsin. Sharp, bitter gusts signaled the coming of an early snowstorm. The wind sent ripples through the stands of spruce and pine, their needle-packed branches waving like layers of fringe. When the air quieted, a twelve-point elk nestled among the trees stopped grazing for a moment. The massive animal raised its antlered head and listened. *Nothing. All good. All safe.* It turned back to the branches and began feasting again.

The winter wind would not stay quiet for long; soon the gusting air roared again, blocking all other sound and causing the cautious animal to freeze in place. A small party of hunters moved stealthily through the fir-filled forest, making their way toward the grazing elk. Buckskin and woolly mammoth hide disguised their scent and protected them from the cold, gusting winds. Standing five and a half feet from hoof to shoulder and weighing more than one thousand pounds, the elk made a very large target, even hidden among the trees. Instinct put the beast on alert, but still it did not hear the spear flying at a whisper toward it. The sound of a cracking branch alerted the massive elk to approaching danger, but it sprang to run too late. The fluted spearhead struck, piercing the animal's reddish brown hide mid-torso. The elk staggered but did not fall. Fear and pain flooded the beast with adrenaline. It quickly recovered its footing and bolted into the woods, leaving the hunters nothing but a view of its cream-colored rump.

The frightened, wounded elk raced through the forest. Its adrenaline-charged speed was no match for the hunters, and they quickly fell behind. The hunters, who needed to feed themselves and their small nomadic tribe during the brutal winter months ahead, knew this huge elk would fill that need for a long time. Losing this kill would be a great disappointment. Luckily, the dusting of snow covering the ground made tracking easy. Hoof prints, broken branches, and blood led their way.

The hunters pursued for a time but then stopped as the first flurries of the threatening snowstorm began to fall. The winds picked up, and the temperature dropped even further. Tracking the elk would be more difficult once fresh snow covered the ground, but the beast had lost a lot of blood, and they knew it would soon fall. The hunting party needed shelter now, so they reluctantly gave up the chase and turned back, empty handed, toward the rock overhang where their tribe made camp.

During the elk's wild run, the spear embedded in its torso caught on the trunk of a large spruce and snapped off. The force of the break drove the spear's fluted stone tip deeper into the animal's flesh. Now weak, the blood-soaked elk struggled to reach the banks of what centuries later would be known as Lost Land Lake. Only its front hoofs touched the cold, soothing water before its slender legs gave way and its massive body crashed to the ground. The elk's twelve-point antlered head, once proudly held high, splashed into the lake water as it died.

Three feet of snow fell during that early winter storm. The new snowpack should have made tracking the elk impossible, but nature gave a gift to the hunting party. Heavy winds blew in the storm's aftermath, leaving high drifts and large patches of bare earth on the forest floor. While searching, the hunters recovered the broken spear staff and quickly tracked the fallen elk to the banks of the nearby lake. The lapping lake water exposed the animal's dark brown head, while its body lay completely covered in snow. Triumphant, the hunting party surrounded the elk, readied their stone tool kits, and butchered the animal where it had fallen.

The nomadic tribe stripped the elk of its meat and hides, left its carcass, and moved on. During the months ahead, hungry animals came to scavenge now and then, dragging off a rib, a hipbone, a vertebra. As ancient Wisconsin left the Ice Age further and further behind, temperatures climbed, glaciers retreated, and lake waters rose. The elk's remains, once resting on the shore, slowly disappeared under the rising waters of Lost Land Lake.

WELCOME BACK

Corbett Griffith III swallowed back the taste of vomit. *Not again*, he moaned, dropping his head between his knees. Wisconsin's County A Highway with its twists, turns, and slopes made his stomach roll and his head ache. *Just like last summer*, Corbett thought miserably. "Could you slow down?" he pleaded from the backseat of the SUV.

His Uncle Dell chuckled. "Carsick, huh? Ride up front. It helps." He gave a nod toward the front passenger seat.

Great, Corbett thought. *Then I can throw up—and get beheaded.* "Can't," he answered aloud, raising his eleven-year-old head slightly. "I'm too small. If the airbag goes off, it'd kill me."

"Oh." Uncle Dell nodded slowly.

Corbett heard the electric whir of the window to his right rolling down, and a fresh breeze filled the backseat. "That helps, too."

Corbett's uncle was smiling at him in the rearview mirror. "Thanks," the boy sighed, giving Dell a halfhearted grin. Corbett stuck his head out the window and took in a few deep breaths. He closed his eyes against the wind that blew through his dark brown hair. *No wonder dogs do this. It feels great.*

And Corbett needed to feel great. He was due. Not much had changed with his family since the previous summer and his first stay at Uncle Dell's Whispering Pines Lodge. *No,* Corbett corrected himself. *It had changed. It had gotten worse.* He had used to be the invisible kid. Now he was the invisible, alone kid. His divorced parents never had had much time for him before, but lately they had no time at all. Corbett's mom, an editor at the *Chicago Sun-Times,* got a promotion that had her working nights, so he really only saw her on weekends. His dad was dating again and traveling more with his job in sales. He was out of the country more than he was in it. Corbett saw him only once or twice a month.

Corbett pulled his head back inside the SUV. His stomach felt a little better. He sat back and absently rubbed the thin, five-inch-long scar running down his left arm. He did that often these days, especially when he felt alone and neglected. Rubbing that scar made him feel better, and he bore it proudly. It was a reminder of the day he had saved a friend, battled a five-foot, seventy-pound muskie and won. The victory had earned Corbett a lot: the Village of Minong's admiration, the fishing community's respect—he was now a master fisherman—and his parents' attention. But the latter, which meant the most to him, hadn't lasted long.

Corbett huffed. His parents didn't even have time to drive him halfway to Whispering Pines like they did the year before.

He'd had to take a bus. *A bus!* Corbett shook his head in disbelief. He had started his summer vacation alone on a bus for four hours. When he saw Uncle Dell—his mother's much older brother—at the Madison bus station, Corbett had never been so happy to see someone in his whole life. *Maybe if that old lady hadn't spent the entire trip sleeping and drooling on my shoulder it would have been OK,* he thought. He had tried several times to push the woman's head away, but she wouldn't budge. Even worse, her hair felt like an S.O.S. pad, and she snored—loudly. Corbett shuddered at the memory.

"Yo! Griffy!"

The cry from outside startled Corbett from his thoughts. *Who was that?*

"Hey! Griff-y!"

Corbett stuck his head out the window again as the SUV approached a culvert. There, at the mouth of the large, metal cylinder, he saw a tall, thin boy with sandy blond hair standing in a kayak and waving a paddle in the air. The boy—and the kayak—wobbled precariously in the small stream flowing through the cylinder.

"Griffy!" the boy called again. He suddenly rocked sharply left and right. "Whoooa," he cried out and dropped from sight.

Corbett smiled as memories flooded back to him. He hadn't been called Griffy since last summer. "Pike!" he yelled, sticking his head farther out the window as the SUV passed by.

Pike popped back up. "Almost lost it," he called after Corbett/ Griffy. "Welcome back, fellow master fisherman. See you at the lodge!"

Corbett waved back wildly, now out of earshot. He kept his head out the window until he could no longer see Pike; then he dropped back into the car. A huge smile filled his face. *Griffy*, he thought and sighed happily. Until that moment, he hadn't realized how much that nickname meant to him. It was a sign that he belonged somewhere, that he was wanted, that he wasn't alone. And at that moment Corbett welcomed his old nickname back, too.

"That boy," Uncle Dell chuckled from the front seat, shaking his crew-cut head of hair. "He's been asking about you all week. 'When's Griffy coming? When are you going to pick him up? How much longer?' I had him clean the fish house three times this week just to keep him occupied."

Griffy grimaced, remembering the bloodstained fish house and its torture chamber–like atmosphere.

"Good thing, too, I see," Uncle Dell laughed as he eyed Griffy in the rearview mirror. "Don't worry, you won't be seeing the inside of the fish house for a week or so. We'll ease you into it."

"Good," Griffy said.

He thought back to last summer, when he had first met Pike McKendrick and thought the boy was nothing but trouble. Pike was a year older than him, and even though his family owned a bait and tackle shop called The Happy Hooker, Pike helped run Uncle Dell's Whispering Pines Lodge instead. Outdoors was where he wanted to be. Dell said Pike had the spirit of an adventurer. To Griffy's surprise, he soon discovered that so did he, and the two boys became fast friends.

"You know, you *can* go faster now," Griffy urged excitedly.

"Yes, sir." Uncle Dell saluted and hit the gas pedal.

The SUV raced deeper and deeper into the Chequamegon National Forest, creating a never-ending blur of white pine and yellow birch trees. Griffy watched eagerly for the sign that would direct them to Peninsula Road. The wild columbine and the surrounding woods often hid the sign from view.

"There it is. There's the sign!" Griffy called out, leaning over the front seat and pointing past Uncle Dell. Dell turned the car quickly, throwing Griffy to the right. "Hey," he cried.

Dell laughed and slowed the car as they bumped down sandy, rocky Peninsula Road. Tree branches scraped and scratched the car as dark, damp woods engulfed them. Griffy, still hanging over the front seat, watched the road ahead. *It's coming. It's coming*, he chanted to himself. The woods slowly pulled back, and there it was: Lost Land Lake. Blue lake water sparkled and danced around them. *Beautiful.*

Uncle Dell stopped the SUV, just as he had done the summer before, in front of two behemoth black bears and the sign the carved animals held high. Griffy glanced up at the faded black letters announcing that this was Whispering Pines Lodge.

"Here we are. Welcome back," Uncle Dell said as the two exited the car. He squeezed Griffy's shoulder. Griffy looked up at him and smiled. "And here comes Pike," Dell said, pointing out to the lake.

Griffy watched as Pike landed his kayak, and then a sharp, excited bark startled him. He turned, looking quizzically around the narrow peninsula that Whispering Pines called home. Out of nowhere, a medium-sized dog with wavy black fur ran toward him.

"Spinner!" Griffy happily called, clapping for the dog to come.

Spinner charged, causing Griffy to instinctively back up. "Whoa. Whoa!" he cried, but the excited animal didn't slow down. Griffy signaled frantically with his hands, but Spinner crashed right into him, swinging his rear end around and checking Griffy in the legs. As Griffy fell to the ground, the dog leaped around him, wagging his tail uncontrollably.

"Well, someone sure missed you." Uncle Dell smiled.

"Me too," Pike chimed in as he ran up to the scene.

"Help!" Griffy called out through bursts of laughter. He couldn't get up with Spinner pouncing on and around him.

"Sorry. On your own," Uncle Dell said with a grin as he turned to unload Griffy's gear from the SUV.

"Here." Pike offered his hand to Griffy. Spinner took the opportunity to check Pike hard in the back of the legs.

"Hey! Spinner, come on," the older boy whined as he crashed to the ground.

The two boys wrestled with Spinner until they were covered with sandy dirt. Pike finally caught the dog by the collar, and the two boys took turns petting him to keep him calm.

"Good boy. Good boy," Griffy said soothingly as he stroked Spinner's fur.

"Wow," Pike exhaled, catching his breath. The three sat in the middle of Peninsula Road, happily exhausted.

"So," Pike began at last. His brown eyes sparkled mischievously. "You up for an adventure?"

Griffy looked at Pike suspiciously. "What do you mean?"

Pike just grinned.

"Seriously. What?" Griffy pleaded.

"I've got big plans for us."

"Really?" Griffy questioned halfheartedly. *Oh, no.* He knew the sparkle in those eyes meant one thing: trouble.

"Yep, really." Pike said. "You're gonna love it."

BIG CROOKED CREEK

Good sleeping, Griffy thought as he stretched out, arms overhead, toes pointed. *Cool and quiet.* He now knew what sleeping like a log meant. He didn't remember moving a muscle the entire night—just sleeping deep under the blankets and deep into the sagging mattress. He quickly moved his arms and legs back and forth under the covers as if making a snow angel and then sat up. Sun streamed in the lodge's loft windows and across his birch log bed. The rays glowed off the antique fishing lures hanging across the room's peaked ceiling and along its wooden walls. A cool morning breeze blew in off Lost Land Lake. The wind played with the curtains, blowing them out into the room and then quickly sucking them back against the window screens again. *It has to be late*, Griffy thought, looking around the room for his watch. Turned out he didn't need one.

"Griffy! Get up," a familiar voice shouted from outside. "It's 9:30 already. Let's go!"

Griffy shuffled barefoot to the window and looked down to see Pike already dressed in swim trunks and a life vest.

"Let's go," Pike yelled again, waving Griffy down. "My dad said we could kayak by ourselves today. Just the two of us."

"I just got up," Griffy whined slightly, "and I'll have to ask Uncle Dell."

"Already done. Geez. Come on."

"I just got up," Griffy repeated. "I haven't even had breakfast."

"Well, grab a Pop-Tart and let's go," Pike answered, shaking his hands impatiently in the air.

Griffy stood there for a moment staring down at his friend. Pike's eyes widened in exasperation, and he tilted his head to one side. *That's a mom look*, Griffy thought. *Definitely a mom look.* The type that said: I'm done, not waiting. Come now, or I'm leaving without you.

Griffy huffed. "Oh, all right. I'm coming."

He was headed for the loft's ladder when he heard Pike order: "Don't worry about brushing your teeth. Just eat something."

Griffy stepped back to the window. "Is it OK if I go to the bathroom?" he asked sarcastically.

"If you must," Pike answered, a grin spreading across his face.

"Thank you." Griffy smiled back and rolled his eyes.

About ten minutes later, Griffy left the lodge in swim trunks, carrying a life vest and munching on a Pop-Tart. Pike had two kayaks waiting. Long-handled butterfly nets stuck out from the seats of both.

"You want to catch butterflies?" Griffy asked skeptically.

"No, frogs and turtles. We're going down Big Crooked Creek."

"Big Crooked Creek?" Griffy chuckled. "Why is it called that?"

"It connects to Big Crooked Lake. I found it on an old map. It's more of a bog than a creek now. That map is so cool. Found it at a flea market. My mom framed it. It's in my room. I'll show you." Griffy opened his mouth, but Pike waved his hand impatiently. "Get in, and I'll push you off."

Griffy settled into his kayak. "Practice paddling here in the bay. You're probably rusty. And check your balance," Pike cautioned as he launched Griffy into the lake. "We're going to be climbing in and out and over things."

"We're going to *what*?" Griffy exclaimed as his kayak glided slowly out into Whispering Pines Bay. He looked back at Pike, panic stricken. He knew Pike did it all the time, but Uncle Dell had told him to never stand in a kayak. It was too dangerous. Uncle Dell had never said anything about climbing out and over things, but Griffy was sure that was a no-no, too.

"It's nothing," Pike said dismissively as he climbed into his own kayak. Still standing, he pushed off the shore with his paddle. Pike smoothly seated himself and effortlessly stroked the cool lake water.

It wasn't going as easily for Griffy. The kayak wobbled and rocked. The paddle slapped the water. *Calm down and get it together*, he told himself. He tried to remember last summer when he had kayaked all over Lost Land Lake with Uncle Dell. He had gotten pretty good at it, or so he thought. Griffy started over, resting the kayak paddle on his knees and sitting still until the kayak was motionless. He closed his eyes and imagined gliding through the water, getting the rhythm in his head. Stroke. Stroke. Stroke.

"What *are* you doing?" Pike asked as he pulled his kayak next to Griffy's. "Wake up."

Griffy just ignored Pike's taunts. When he was ready, he opened his eyes and paddled smoothly through the water. Stroke. Stroke. Stroke. Stroke.

"Hey, that's it!" Pike marveled as Griffy glided away. "You've got it."

"Yes, I do." Griffy smiled, very pleased with himself.

"Don't get too cocky there, dude." Pike shook his head in amusement and then motioned toward the lake with it. "So let's go. Follow me."

The two paddled out of Whispering Pines Bay following the tree- and brush-lined shore past Twin Pines to the tip of the peninsula and finally to Shallow Pass. The graying sky, the calm water, and the still air gave the morning a serene feel that Griffy didn't want to disturb. Mother Nature quietly demanded their respect, and she got it. Both boys were unusually quiet. Finally, Pike slowed his kayak and signaled for Griffy to pull up beside him.

"We're going in there," he whispered, pointing across Shallow Pass to a grassy area covered in lily pads.

Griffy squinted, scanning the area. "In where? I don't see an opening."

"It's there. Come on."

Griffy followed Pike again as he paddled into Shallow Pass. Shore to shore, this section of the lake was not even a quarter mile wide, and the water here was only two feet deep. Last summer Griffy had been amazed at how he could walk from the point of the peninsula to the opposite shoreline with the water never reaching his waist. Now, he peered over the side of his kayak and studied the lake's sandy bottom. Minnows darted around. Specks of algae drifted here and there.

At the center of the pass, yellow pond lilies and green pads dotted the lake's surface. As the two kayaks neared the far shore, a startled heron took flight. The bird, nearly invisible in a thick of fallen tree limbs, rose up with one flap of its large wings. Its pointy bill led the way, while its long, skinny legs floated effortlessly behind it.

As the boys paddled on, soon the lily pads gave way to clusters of thick, spiny grass. They kayaked along this weedy border until Pike suddenly turned and disappeared into the brush. Griffy followed and found himself in a narrow channel lined by walls of grass and reeds. He struggled to paddle as the grasses clogged more and more of the kayak's path. *Where are we going?* he wondered. He didn't like this channel one bit. Reeds and weeds slithered across his arms and whipped his face. Insects assaulted him. The small pockets of water he passed rippled with movement as creatures too quick for him to see leaped away from the slow-moving kayak. He was very afraid something—he didn't know exactly what—would jump or fall into his kayak. Then, to his relief, he saw the grasses ahead pulling back. The channel opened up, and the boys found themselves paddling into a small, secluded pond.

Pike glided into the middle of the pond and turned his kayak back to face Griffy. "Cool, huh?"

"Cool," Griffy agreed, looking around. The pond was surrounded by a maze of channels and weed-choked water pockets. Dead trees and driftwood lay haphazardly around.

Turtles and frogs sunned themselves on the fallen branches. The stagnant pond had the smell of death and decay. It was eerie, a place forgotten. If not for the brightly colored wild irises and thistles dotting its borders, the pond would have been all gloom and doom, Griffy observed.

"There's more," Pike said in a hushed voice. "Follow me." He turned and maneuvered down one of the winding, weed-clogged channels.

The channel split and forked several times. Griffy tried very hard to pay attention to their path, noting a landmark here and there. He didn't want to get lost out here; Griffy didn't trust that Pike knew where they were going, much less how to get back. How could anyone remember all these twists and turns? Everything looked the same.

Pike signaled for Griffy to stop. "This is it," he announced, his voice still hushed. "Beaver dam."

Griffy peered around Pike's kayak and saw that the channel dead-ended at a mound of branches and mud that rose about three feet above the water. "We're going up and over," Pike announced.

"What?" Griffy blurted out loudly, breaking the quiet the boys had been observing. "No way."

"Yes way. Just do what I do. It's easy."

Paddling with strong, deep strokes, Pike crashed his kayak into the dam. The force of the impact drove the tip of the kayak about halfway up the dam's side. With the boat anchored there, Pike stood up and carefully stepped out onto the dam. He pulled his kayak over the branches so it was lodged on the other side of the dam and then climbed back in. Pike held his paddle overhead and with back and forth movements scooted himself all the way into the water on the other side, vanishing.

Griffy sat in his kayak a few yards from the beaver dam and waited for further direction, maybe a call from Pike to hurry up. Something. Anything. But there was nothing.

He yelled out, "Hey."

Nothing.

"Pike! Hey!"

Nothing.

"Where are you?"

Nothing.

Great. Now what? Griffy really didn't trust himself to get over that dam, and the last thing he wanted to do was fall into the stagnant, murky goo surrounding him while trying. *I could sit here until Pike returns, but who knows how long that will be?* Griffy had thought this creek-turned-bog was creepy with Pike, but it was even creepier without him. He peered into the greenish brown water. *There have to be leeches in there. Just have to be.* Something stirred in the water behind him. He quickly whipped his head around but saw nothing. Letting out a long, weary huff, he decided he was not going to sit here surrounded by creepy, crawly, slithering things all by himself. Griffy paddled as fast and as hard as he could toward the dam.

Boom! He hit the dam just as Pike had. Slowly, cautiously, Griffy stood up. He struggled for balance, found it, and then slowly stepped one foot onto the dam. He straddled the side of the kayak in a squat, and using his paddle as leverage, he pulled his other leg out and onto the dam. *That wasn't so bad,* he thought. Griffy hauled his kayak onto the top of the beaver's home just as his friend had done. The dam's branches cracked and groaned under his weight.

It's like a land of the lost, he thought in awe as he faced what lay on the other side. It was another pond—a deathly quiet, deathly still pond much larger than the one they had left and shaped in a nearly perfect circle. Standing on tiptoe straining for a look, Griffy saw a single channel leading off. There was no sign of Pike, but that had to be where he'd gone.

Griffy angled his kayak toward the pond and, grabbing the sides with both hands, he stepped one leg in. But as he was lifting the other leg, the kayak suddenly slipped. Griffy gasped as he and the kayak slid toward the water. Panicked, he forced his leg down, hoping to get it in the kayak. Instead, he let out a painful cry as his leg cracked through the tangle of branches and muck, sinking shin-deep into the beaver dam. Gritting his teeth, he tried to pull his leg out, but the kayak slid even farther down the dam, forcing him into the half splits. He couldn't move.

"Help!" Griffy cried out. "Pike, help." He waited, but there was no response. He yelled again, as loud as he could. "Pike! Help!"

Once more, he heard nothing.

Griffy's lips quivered. He tried to control his fear but couldn't. *No one is ever there for me. No one.* He began sobbing. *I'm always alone, always neglected, always invisible.* Tears rolled down his face, and his whole body shook. He stayed that way—sniffling and stuck in the half splits—for several moments. Then, through the blur of tears, the scar on his arm caught his attention. He stared at it. Images of a monster muskie with two-inch, razor-sharp teeth filled his mind. He had fought that beast and won.

Griffy shook his head sharply side to side. *Enough*, he scolded himself. *Big baby. Crying isn't going to help you.*

Just then, the water at the base of the dam rippled with movement. *What was that?* Griffy's tears dried up quickly as he snapped to attention. He stared cautiously at the rippling water. *Please go away. Please go away. Whatever you are, please go away.* His stomach tightened with fear. Griffy watched helplessly as two long antennae poked out of the water. A rusty red head with beady, black eyes soon emerged, as did two very large pincers. Griffy gasped. *It's some sort of mutant lobster.* Repulsed, he desperately tried to pull back. It was no use. He was stuck. The creature, not paying any attention to Griffy before, took full notice of him now. It flicked its flipper-like tail up and down and raised its pincers as if readying for a fight.

Oh, crap.

Griffy looked down, taking note of his very vulnerable position. And the area that was most vulnerable—well, it wasn't a good one.

Suddenly, with spider-like speed, the creature charged at him.

Oh, crap. Oh, crap. Oh, crap. Griffy's heart raced. Adrenaline pumped through his body. He looked frantically around. The kayak paddle was just out of reach, but there was a thick branch sticking up out of the dam. Using all his muscle power, Griffy pulled the branch free and swung. He hit the creature just in time, knocking it back into the water. *Yes! Take that, mutant lobster*, Griffy congratulated himself, but then he watched in shock as the creature quickly resurfaced and, as if jet propelled, sped through the water back at him.

"Hey, what are you yelling about over here?" Pike called as he glided out of the channel and reentered the pond. "I almost caught this really cool …" He stopped short, silenced by the scene before him. "Hang on, Grif! I'm coming."

Pike sprang to action, paddling hard and fast toward his friend, but there was no time to wait for rescue. Griffy planted the branch firmly back into the dam and used it as leverage to hoist the kayak closer in an effort to get at least one of his legs mobile. But the muck covering the dam was too slippery. The kayak moved just a little, then slid back, moved a little, then slid back. With the branch stuck in the beaver dam again, Griffy had nothing to protect himself from the ugly crazed creature as it scurried in for a second attack. He smacked it away with the only weapon he had—his hands—but the creature was quick, very quick. It caught the side of Griffy's hand in one of its sharp claws and clamped down hard. Griffy winced.

"Owww!" he cried, shaking his hand violently. Pike's kayak crashed into the dam with a thud, and Pike started to stand up. Griffy kept shaking. "Let go. Let go. Let …" and with the last shake, the creature flew off his hand and hit Pike squarely in the chest, "… go!" Griffy finished as Pike yelped, lost his balance, and crashed backward into the murky, muddy water.

Griffy held his breath until he saw his friend surface. "Look out, Pike. That thing is in the water." He pointed frantically. "There! There! See it?"

Pike did. He kept his eyes glued on it. As its thrusting tail propelled it forward, he grabbed it behind its two large claws and snatched it up out of the water.

Griffy's mouth dropped open. *How'd he do that?*

"It's just a crawdad," Pike announced, holding the creature up for Griffy to see.

"A what?"

"You know, a crawdad."

Griffy shook his head. He was from Chicago, and he was pretty sure there weren't crawdads in Chicago.

Pike turned the creature over, examining it from every side. "It's the biggest I've ever seen. He's got to be at least six inches long. And really aggressive, too. I'm keeping him."

"What do you mean, keeping him? As a pet?" Griffy questioned in disbelief. "That thing attacked me. It was coming in for the kill."

Pike snickered as he dropped the crawdad into his kayak and then waded over to Griffy.

"Come on, Grif. He's six inches long. You could step on him and squish him dead."

Griffy gave Pike a look of indignation. "In case you didn't notice, I'm kinda stuck here."

Pike rubbed his chin. "Yeah, how *did* you do that?"

That question and the sight of Pike standing, as calm as could be, knee-deep in muck with beads of black goo dripping off him, forced a reluctant snort out of Griffy. But then relief washed over him. The snort turned into a snicker, and the two boys burst into full-out laughter as they worked to free Griffy's leg.

"I don't know how," Griffy finally answered. He examined his blood-streaked shin and shrugged. "Just happened. Besides, you left me."

"Good Gouda, dude, I thought you were right behind me. And I didn't think you of all people would need help," Pike stated, matter-of-factly.

Griffy chuckled to himself. He had forgotten how Pike and his sister, Gil, used cheese as expletives or curse words. "You saved me from a monster muskie, remember?" Pike said.

Griffy nodded sheepishly.

"But now," Pike continued, grinning ear to ear, "we're even Stevens, 'cause I just saved *you* from a killer crawdad."

"Even Stevens?" Griffy questioned. "I don't think so. That muskie was five feet long. Five feet! Not six inches. Five feet!" He spread his arms wide in the air to emphasize his point.

"Whatever," Pike retorted, and the two argued and teased each other all the way back to Whispering Pines.

The boys' adventure down Big Crooked Creek had left them both covered in stagnant, smelly black goo. With one look at the two, Uncle Dell shooed them off the lodge's porch. "Don't even think about coming in here like that," he scolded. "What on earth happened out there?"

"Long story," Griffy replied quickly, brushing off the question. His leg had stopped bleeding, and his hand had stopped throbbing. He didn't look any worse than Pike usually did, bringing him to the sad conclusion that he had overreacted out on Big Crooked Creek. He was a little embarrassed by it.

Uncle Dell's voice brought him back to the present. "Look at you. Is that supposed to be camouflage? You both look like you've just stepped out of the bush in Vietnam."

"Yep," Pike answered, "and we brought back a POW." He held up the crawdad.

Uncle Dell's eyes widened. "That's the biggest crawdad I've ever seen." His tone quickly changed. "You keep a hold of that, Pike," he warned, shaking a finger at the mischievous boy. "I don't want to hear a word from any guests about that crawdad."

"Yes, sir," Pike saluted. "He's going in one of the bait tanks at The Happy Hooker."

"Good. Now stay right there—both of you."

Uncle Dell disappeared into the lodge. When he returned, he had a bar of soap and two towels.

"Go clean up in the lake. I don't want to see either of you until that black goo is gone."

✳   ✳   ✳   ✳

At breakfast the next morning, Griffy sat groggily at the table. He hadn't slept well at all, tossing and turning and itching all night. Even now, he couldn't stop scratching. His skin prickled and burned. Uncle Dell noticed this as he served up a stack of pancakes. "Bites?" he asked.

Griffy nodded.

"Let's have a look."

Griffy lifted his pajama top. A ring of red welts circled his abdomen.

"Duck itch," Uncle Dell announced. "I'll get the calamine lotion."

"What itch?" Griffy called after him.

"Duck," Uncle Dell answered as he reentered the kitchen. He dotted the soothing pink lotion across Griffy's stomach. "Comes from flatworm parasites in the lake. Ducks are carriers. The parasites bury themselves in your skin. Itch like a ..." He stopped and looked hesitantly at Griffy. "Well, bad."

"I've got parasites?" Griffy grimaced, looking at his stomach in disgust.

Uncle Dell chuckled. "You must have picked it up when you were bathing in the lake. It'll go away in a few days. No worries."

Griffy stared warily at his rash. *No worries?* He thought of the movie *Aliens* and pictured creatures suddenly exploding out of his body. "W-w-where do the parasites go?" he stammered.

Uncle Dell chuckled again. "Nowhere. Your body killed them. Turns out you aren't a good host."

"Oh," the boy answered quietly, still a little sickened at the thought. Dell tousled Griffy's hair and went back to the stove, still chuckling. Griffy eyed his stomach again and cautiously poked at the red welts. *Great, they're dead in there. That's so much better.*

THE REDHEADS

"The Redheads are coming," Pike announced with disgust, slamming the Whispering Pines reservation book shut. He and Griffy were hanging out in the lodge's lobby eating Popsicles and snooping around.

Griffy stood on tiptoe nearby, straining for a better view of the large elk head mounted high on the lodge's stone fireplace. The animal's neck angled to the left to show off its long, backward-sweeping antlers. Elk were ugly, Griffy decided, not cute at all, like deer. The elk looked more like a bull, only with antlers. He forgot about the Popsicle in his hand until he felt cold liquid running down his arm. He quickly licked up the melting mess before it dripped all over the floor.

"Who are the Redheads?" he asked in between licks. "I don't remember them from last year."

"They didn't come up," Pike answered. "Death in the family. Bad for them. Very good for us. They are slobs. And I don't think any of them weighs under three hundred pounds."

Still licking, Griffy shrugged. "So?"

"So," Pike replied, "come Saturday, you and me will be doing nothing but cleaning up after those guys. Garbage patrol. Every day. All week. Got it?" Pike finished off his Popsicle with one final bite and lobbed the stick into a nearby garbage can. It clanked loudly as if emphasizing his point.

Griffy nodded that he got it, but he really didn't. *How bad could they be?*

A few days later, the round and redheaded Reakes clan wasted no time answering Griffy's question. The six-member family settled in to Cabin 9 around 5:00 PM Saturday. That night, loud clanking and clanging in the darkness outside woke Griffy up—repeatedly. Having no idea what was making all that noise, he eventually got up to see. Moving hesitantly toward the loft's window, he strained to see whatever was out there. Finally his nose pushed against the window's screen. Then he saw it: a large shadow moved stealthily among the trees. Griffy sprang back. That was it for him. *Don't know what that is. Don't want to know what that is.* He raced back to his bed, jumped in, buried himself deep in the covers, and stayed there.

Sunday morning, just as Pike had predicted, the two boys found themselves on garbage patrol. Coffee grounds, apple cores, candy wrappers, spaghetti, and soggy paper towels littered the ground around Cabin 9. Darlene Reakes explained with no apology that her son, Dewey, had taken the garbage out the night before. Annoyed at having to do the chore, the sixteen-year-old had simply dropped the overstuffed sacks into the metal

25

trash can outside the cabin and walked away, not bothering to replace the lid or properly secure it to the can, as Griffy knew he was instructed to do. Uncle Dell equipped all the resort's garbage cans with bungee straps to keep the lids on tight and prowling bears at bay. Without the straps, Uncle Dell warned, the twelve Whispering Pines cabins would offer hungry black bears a nightly smorgasbord of treats.

Wearily surveying the grounds, Griffy now knew what had kept him up all night: bears, frustrated bears, wrestling one Whispering Pines garbage can after another. Obviously encouraged by the feast put out for them at Cabin 9, they'd hit every cabin. Pike and Griffy found Cabin 7's trash can rolled down the hill and wrapped around a birch tree. They located Cabin 4's floating in the lake. Cabin 8's can was just gone. The boys searched and searched but couldn't find it anywhere.

"This stinks," Pike grumbled as he and Griffy cleaned up around Cabin 9 later that morning.

"In more ways than one," Griffy grimaced as he picked up a sticky wad of tissues. "This is grossing me out. I don't even want to know what's on these." He held his black garbage bag at arm's length as he dropped the clump in.

"Ha! Look at you two," came a mocking shout from Cabin 9's screened porch. It was Dewitt, the youngest Reakes boy. "All you need are capes and you could be superheroes." He came outside and posed regally with his hands on his hips. "Can Man and Rubbish," Dewitt proclaimed loudly. "Where's your trash-mobile?" The boy began laughing himself silly.

Pike simply rolled his eyes. "Good Gouda, you're a riot," he deadpanned.

Griffy knew he and his friend looked funny; no one needed to tell him that. Dell had sent the boys to work in T-shirts; shorts; tall, yellow muck boots; and bright blue dish gloves.

Dwade Reakes followed his younger brother outside to join the fun. He was eating from a box of doughnuts and sprayed crumbs and powdered sugar as he laughed. Dewitt grabbed a doughnut and threw it on the ground. "Hey, Can Man! You missed something," he taunted.

For twelve-year-old Pike, that was enough. "Come on, Grif. We're done here." Carrying garbage bags over their shoulders, he and Griffy walked away, leaving Dewitt and Dwade laughing hysterically behind them.

✳ ✳ ✳ ✳

Early Monday morning, Griffy climbed down the loft's ladder still half asleep, his brown hair matted in clumps against his head. He needed to pee.

"Good, you're up," Uncle Dell called from the kitchen. "I've got a job for you. Pike'll be here at eight."

"Huh?" Griffy asked, puzzled. He squinted against the morning sunlight, standing perched on the ladder's last rung. It was too much information, too early.

"Wake up, boy!" Uncle Dell ordered with a chuckle. Then he explained, "There's a mess on the beach we need to clean up ASAP."

Griffy's fog started to lift. "The beach?" He still clung to the ladder with one hand, scratching his uncombed head of hair with the other. "Who on earth is on the beach?"

"*Was* on the beach," Uncle Dell corrected. "Last night. I'll give you one guess."

"Sweet Brie," Griffy sighed as he dropped to the floor. "The Redheads."

✳ ✳ ✳ ✳

Not half an hour later, Pike and Griffy stood on the patchy lawn surrounding Whispering Pines's manmade beach. Golden, pebbled sand led down to the lapping lake water and followed the shoreline in a fifteen- by ten-foot swath. Over the years, small tufts of grass had invaded its borders, slowly blending beach and lawn together. The fish-cleaning house sat kitty-corner a few yards away. A plank dock led out from the beach into the water, its square shape creating an enclosed swimming area in the bay. The boys, once again wearing high muck boots and dish gloves, surveyed the damage.

"Holy chedda' cheese." Griffy's blue eyes dulled with disgust. "What a mess."

All eight of the lodge's metal lawn chairs, stacked neatly the night before, now were scattered about. One was half buried in the sand. Two were submerged in the lake. If that wasn't enough, pop cans and empty chip bags littered the damp shoreline. Grit and mulch from discarded bait cartons dirtied the dock. Cigarette butts floated throughout the swim area.

"Don't they sleep?" Griffy asked. He'd gone to bed around 10:30 the night before and had seen no one near the beach. "Why would they be out here so late? What could they possibly have been doing? Why does Uncle Dell put up with this? Why would …"

28

"OK, OK," Pike soothed, interrupting Griffy's rant. "Mr. Redhead is an old Army buddy of Dell's. I guess they go way back. And catfishing. They were catfishing. Catfish come in to feed late at night. This bay is good for it."

"Oh," Griffy answered flatly, and then his eyes widened as realization hit. "Ohhh, nooo," he whined. Fishing meant fish cleaning. He looked warily over at the fish house, dreading going into that smelly, insect-infested place.

Pike smirked. "Ohhh, yes. And it's going to be bad. Trust me. Catfish are skinned."

"Skinned?"

Pike nodded.

"Alive?"

"Sometimes."

The color drained from Griffy's face. Pike patted him reassuringly on the shoulder. "We'll save the fish house for last. OK?"

The boys were well into the cleanup when a Department of Natural Resources boat entered the bay. They stopped working and watched it. Since the previous summer's muskie attacks, the DNR had patrolled Lost Land Lake frequently. Griffy heard the boat's motor idle down as it turned toward the swimming dock.

"Great," Pike whispered. "He's coming over."

The DNR stopping by to chat was never a good thing, Griffy knew. A few days ago, Hannah Brown from Cabin 12 had caught a three-pound smallmouth bass off the dock. The problem was, bass weren't in season yet. Excited, she'd decided to keep the fish just to show it off. It was a bad idea and bad timing. The DNR pulled up just then and fined her for having an illegal bass in her possession. She wasn't going to keep it, she explained. She'd just wanted to show it to her husband. The DNR ranger didn't care. Illegal possession was illegal possession, he said sternly. Furious, Hannah had vowed never to return to Lost Land Lake again.

"So, how are my two favorite master fishermen?" the ranger called.

The "he" turned out to be a "she;" it was DNR ranger Jo Patterson, who'd helped keep last summer's Master Fisherman Muskie Competition under control.

"Jo!" Griffy called out, waving.

Pike smiled and waved, too, as Jo cut the motor and let the boat glide up to the dock.

"Nice to see you back in the Dairy State, Griffy." She looked the two boys up and down. They had been wading through the swim area scooping up cigarette butts and soggy potato chips. "Well, you two are quite a sight. What's this mess from?"

"Guests," Pike said bluntly.

Jo nodded. "Of course. Good to see Dell is on top of things. I won't have to fine you." She winked. "Now I know why this bay is attracting so many ducks. Food supply. You've got three families in here now." She pointed to the clusters of ducks and ducklings along the bay. "Watch out for duck itch!"

"We already had it," Griffy sighed. "Last week. A few bites. It wasn't too bad."

"Well, this summer's water temperature is higher than normal, so it's going to get bad," Jo warned. "And if all these host ducks stick around, it's going to get *really* bad in this bay."

"That's just great," Pike grumbled. "Another thing the Redheads have ruined. We'll never be able to go swimming now."

"Oh, you can swim," Jo corrected. "You just have to take precautions. If you really want to swim, baby oil's your answer."

"Baby oil?" Griffy questioned.

"Sure. The key to stopping duck itch is to keep the water from drying on your body. That's when the parasites penetrate the skin." She lightly pinched Pike's arm for emphasis. "Oil repels water. Just keep your body slathered in baby oil, dry off really well, and you'll be fine."

Pike rubbed his arm as if Jo had hurt him. He mock-pouted at her, then grinned. "We'll try it. Right, Grif?"

Griffy nodded. "Thanks for the tip."

"No problem." Jo pushed the boat away from the dock and started the motor. "You two have a good day. Say hi to Dell, and I'll be seeing you."

The boys waved good-bye as Jo continue on her morning patrol.

"So, Can Man," Pike teased, "interested in saving Whispering Pines from the evil Redheads?"

Griffy saw a familiar sparkle in Pike's brown eyes and knew that the Redheads were in for some big trouble. Usually that mischievous look made Griffy very nervous, but this time he didn't hesitate to say, "I'm in."

GOOD RIDDANCE, REDHEADS

Pike and Griffy kept Jo's baby oil remedy a sworn secret, but they did pass on her duck itch warning. Uncle Dell quickly posted a "Swim at Your Own Risk" sign in the middle of the Whispering Pines beach. Sure enough, the threat of angry, itching red welts that could cause weeks of agony kept guests out of the water.

Atypical for northern Wisconsin, the sun came out early on Wednesday and stayed out, beating down brightly on Lost Land Lake. Temperatures hovered near ninety. Griffy smiled happily up at the sky, seeing not one cloud. That smile never left his face as he walked the Whispering Pines grounds in search of whatever mess awaited the boys today. Severed catfish heads? Gooey, slimy trash? Griffy didn't care. He and Pike couldn't have asked for better weather conditions for their plans. It was hot, and the cabins at Whispering Pines were not air conditioned.

Since cooling off in the lake was out of the question, most guests had already left the resort for the day in search of other ways to stay cool.

Around 1:00 PM, the bell on the lodge's door clanked loudly as all six members of the large and sweaty Reakes clan entered. They lumbered their way to the reception desk, where Dewey impatiently smacked the bell sitting on the counter until Uncle Dell appeared from his adjoining office. He had been taking advantage of the hot day by spending it indoors doing paperwork in the only air-conditioned room at the lake. Just as Dell entered the lobby, Pike and Griffy slipped into his office to eavesdrop through the partially closed door.

"What can I do for you all?" Dell asked.

"Looking to rent a pontoon for the afternoon," Dwayne, the dad, replied. "Know a good place? The family's dying in this heat."

"Popsicles, Dad. Popsicles," Dwade nagged.

"And Popsicles. Give us four Popsicles," the dad added.

Dell got the treats out of the freezer and handed one to each Reakes child, who in turn grabbed them, unwrapped them and threw the wrappers on the floor.

"Put those in the garbage," Darlene instructed when she saw the shocked look on Dell's face. "You know better." But none of the kids paid her any attention, and Darlene made no move to pick the wrappers up herself. She simply shrugged and smiled sheepishly at Dell.

He frowned, but let it pass. "For renting," he said, "Sleepy Eye is the most convenient. It's just down the peninsula here."

As Dell and Dwayne discussed pontoon rentals, Pike and Griffy put on their swim trunks, grabbed their swim towels, and snuck outside through the kitchen door. They cut across the lodge's patchy front lawn, where the Reakes kids now meandered about licking their Popsicles. Pike and Griffy ignored them and headed straight for the beach.

Pike dropped his towel on a lawn chair, kicked off his flips flops, ran to the end of the dock, and dove in. Griffy followed close behind but hesitated at the dock's edge. "Come on in, Grif," Pike encouraged. "It's great!"

Griffy thought twice, not wanting to feel the shock from a jolt of cold water. Instead he turned around and headed back to the beach. As he walked down the dock, a sly grin surfaced briefly on his face. All four Reakes kids, standing along Peninsula Road, had taken notice of him.

"Hey! Where are you going?" Pike yelled from the lake. He bounced up and down trying to see over the dock. The water hit right under his chin. "I said, the water's great."

Griffy ignored him and grabbed one of the inner tubes looped over the wooden stake at the dock. Seeing this, Pike called out, "Hey! Get me one, too."

Griffy did and, pushing the inner tubes in front of him, he slowly waded out, getting used to the water temperature as he went. Pike swam over and took a tube.

"You wimp," he teased, pouncing on Griffy, trying to dunk him under the water. But the oil covering Griffy's body made it impossible for Pike to hold on. The younger boy slipped away, and Pike ended up dunking himself.

"Ha! That'll teach you to mess with me," Griffy laughed.

"You are sooo lucky," Pike taunted.

The two then tried to hoist themselves onto their inner tubes, but they slid off again and again. Pike finally managed to get himself onto his, but Griffy, weak from laughter, couldn't do it. Pike had to hold Griffy's inner tube steady while he plopped himself in butt first off the dock.

Pike rolled his eyes as Griffy got comfortable in the tube. "Good Gouda, it's about time."

"Race you to the end of the dock," Griffy challenged, and the two boys kicked and splashed out into the lake.

All the commotion and obvious fun the boys were having finally got the best of Dewey, Dwade, Dewitt, and Darla. The shaking dock and their loud thuds on it drew Pike and Griffy's attention. They stopped splashing and just floated lazily in the water.

"Yes?" Pike questioned impatiently as he looked up at the Redheads. "Do you want something?"

"I thought the water was off limits?" Dewey demanded, half questioning.

"Yeah," Darla chimed in, pointing. "There's a sign."

"Yes," Griffy answered, "and it says 'Swim at Your Own Risk.' We're risking it."

"You'll get duck itch," Dewitt countered.

"Duck itch, smuck itch," Pike retorted. "We don't care about no stinking duck itch."

"Yeah," Griffy agreed. "That's for babies. Just a few little bites, that's all. See." He pointed to a now-small welt on his stomach from the Big Crooked Creek misadventure. Pike showed off similar welts on his arms.

"That's it? That's duck itch?" Dwade asked in disbelief. "That's nothing."

"That's what we're telling ya," Pike replied with a look and tone that clearly added, "you big dummies."

"Uncle Dell likes to play it safe," Griffy explained. "Doesn't want any complaints from guests. He's cautious. But really all you have to do is dry off good."

With this, Dewey, Dwade, Dewitt, and Darla had heard enough. They dropped their Popsicle sticks where they stood and thudded off the dock toward the resort. In no time at all, the four emerged from Cabin 9 suited up and ready to swim.

"Here they come," Pike announced with a snicker. "Let's get out of here."

The boys hustled themselves into hiding just before the fair-skinned, freckle-covered quartet plunged into the lake. Minutes later, Dwayne and Darlene exited the lodge to find their children frolicking happily in the cool lake water.

"Out of the water, kids," Darlene ordered.

"No way!" the quartet cried.

"You heard your mother, now *out*!" Dwayne commanded.

"In!" the quartet shouted together.

"You'll get duck itch," Darlene warned.

"Duck itch, smuck itch," the kids mocked.

Their parents gave up. "Fine, then," Dwayne announced. "Your mother and I are renting a pontoon. We'll be back at five. Be out by then and ready for dinner. And boys." They paid him no attention. "*Boys!*" Dwayne shouted angrily. Dewey, Dwade, and Dewitt finally stopped jumping in and out of the water and gave their father their full attention. "Watch your sister."

They impatiently nodded before cannonballing off the dock onto Darla's raft. She shrieked loudly as it capsized.

Pike and Griffy, laughing themselves silly, snuck back into the lodge. The lake water rolled off their baby oil-coated bodies in beads. Still, to be safe, they showered and toweled off thoroughly.

"This oil won't come off," Pike complained when he emerged from the bathroom, a towel wrapped around his waist.

"I know," Griffy stated. "I still feel oily." He hoped his towel would absorb more of the oil. He thought for a moment. "Hey, we used baby oil to repel the water. How about baby powder to soak it up? I think I saw some in one of the cabinets."

"It's worth a try," Pike agreed.

The boys took turns covering themselves from head to toe with baby powder.

"Ahhh. That felt good," Griffy sighed when he finished.

"Yeah, but I feel like I've just been prepped for the frying pan," Pike laughed.

Griffy looked at his now-white torso and the powder-covered floor. "Sweet Brie. We've been dipped and coated," he snickered.

"Bawk! Bawk!" Pike cackled, and he strutted like a chicken down the hall.

"Shhh," Griffy scolded. "Quit messing around. Uncle Dell will hear you. Get back here and help me clean this up."

Still coated, the boys dressed, gave the floor a quick wipe with their towels and then went to hang out in the lodge's lobby.

"There you are," Uncle Dell announced as he entered the room through his office door. "What's with the powder?" He leaned over the reception counter and pointed to a white trail leading across the lobby floor. "I've been tracking you two all through the lodge."

Oops, Griffy thought as he fiddled with the TV dial trying to find a static-free station on the ancient set. Pike, sipping a cold Coke, had plopped himself into an overstuffed chair. "Oh, just trying to stay cool," Griffy answered.

Uncle Dell looked at their ghost-white limbs. He squinted suspiciously. "That's all, huh?"

"Yep," Griffy and Pike said in unison, nodding their heads innocently.

✳ ✳ ✳ ✳

Dwade woke in the early morning hours to the pinch of something biting him. He sluggishly slapped his arm. "Ow," he moaned and started scratching.

In the bed next to him, Dewitt woke up scratching, too. "Dang mosquitoes keep biting me," he complained.

"Me too," Dwade replied. The two pulled the sheets over their heads and buried themselves in the covers for protection.

Down the hall, Dewey and Darla tossed and turned in their rooms, also. Their prickly skin itched madly. Hot, sweaty, and flushed, Darla finally got up to seek comfort from her mother. Standing in the dark at the side of her parents' bed, she shook her mother awake. "I'm sick," she whined. "I hurt—all over."

Darlene took her daughter into the bathroom, turned on the light, and screamed in shock. Bright red welts dotted her daughter's sweaty, swollen face. Darlene frantically examined the rest of Darla's body only to find welts, some the size of golf balls, covering her entire body.

"They itch," Darla moaned just as her father entered the bathroom.

"What's wro ..." Dwayne stopped mid-question and gasped at the sight of his daughter.

Darla began to scratch. "Don't!" her mother scolded.

"But I itch!"

"So do I." Dwayne and Darlene turned to find Dewey standing drowsily before them, scratching his red, swollen arms.

"Go check on Dewitt and Dwade," Darlene instructed her husband.

Soon every light in Cabin 9 burned bright as mother and father tried to soothe their children's agonizing itching. They finally loaded everyone up into their car and drove forty-five minutes to the nearest emergency room.

Pike and Griffy never saw the Redheads again that year. It turned out that they were extremely susceptible to duck itch. Griffy learned from Uncle Dell that their cases were the worst the emergency room staff had ever seen. The doctor said the only cure was time—possibly several weeks. He'd prescribed antihistamines and calamine lotion and sent them back to Whispering Pines. Without air conditioning, however, the cabins were too unbearable for the feverish clan. The family packed up and left the next day.

That afternoon, Uncle Dell sent Pike and Griffy over to Cabin 9 to strip the beds and collect the linens. "You two did something," he reprimanded. "I don't know what, but when I find out ... well ..." Dell hesitated.

Beads of sweat broke out across Griffy's forehead. He fidgeted and nervously looked at Pike. He just knew they were done for. But surprisingly, Uncle Dell chuckled. He rubbed his graying hair. "Oh, just go," he finally ordered, shoving laundry baskets at them.

Relief washed over Griffy. He and Pike practically danced all the way to Cabin 9. "Good riddance, Redheads," they exclaimed, high-fiving victoriously.

FAME AND GLORY, PART I

Dr. Emmett Potts of the University of Wisconsin–Madison sat in his field tent on Big Crooked Lake. Hands clasped behind his head, he leaned back in his chair and swiveled around. The tent's untied door flapped lazily in the wind, exposing a group of archaeology students busily at work outside. Dr. Potts looked out at them in disappointment. He had spent three summers supervising digs on the Ojibwe Indian Reservation, and so far the sites had produced nothing. Sure, they found the occasional arrowhead, clay pot, or cooking utensil, but they'd discovered nothing of significance, nothing to make a career, nothing to earn him fame and glory. Emmett knew that small, nomadic tribes had roamed, hunted, and lived in this area during the Ice Age. Artifacts dating back ten thousand years or more were out there. They had to be. All his research pointed to it. He wanted a find, needed a find, expected a find—but so far, nothing.

"Professor Potts." A young, eager face poked through the tent opening. "We've unearthed some stoneware."

It's Dr. Potts, he huffed to himself, but he nodded slowly and said, "I'll be right there."

Emmett turned back to his desk and heaved out a weary sigh. No respect, not even from his students. He had earned his doctorate degree years ago, but still it was always *Professor* Potts. Professor Potts with a long, un-storied career. He was in his mid sixties, and he knew talk was circulating through the anthropology department about his retirement. But he couldn't retire—he wouldn't retire—not without the fame and glory he deserved.

Stoneware, he muttered bitterly. *How exciting*.

Emmett Potts slowly pushed himself up out of his chair and left the tent.

THE STORM

The porch door at Whispering Pines Lodge slammed shut as Griffy ran outside. Fishing pole in one hand and tackle box in the other, he scurried quickly down to the banks of Whispering Pines Bay. Bass were finally in season, and he couldn't wait to get out on the lake. Having been stuck up in the lodge's kitchen drying dinner dishes, it had been near torture listening to all the laughter and shouting going on down at the dock as Uncle Dell, Pike, and Mitch McKendrick, Pike's dad, readied the boat.

Griffy ran faster before coming to an abrupt stop at the head of the dock. Pike's sister, Gil, approached, carrying a fish basket and a couple cans of Coke. "You coming, too?" Griffy asked.

"Yep. It's going to be one crowded boat. Try not to cast over my line."

Griffy's face dropped in disappointment. Gil, now fifteen, got bossier by the day. She stared contemptuously at him, her eyes moving up to the hat he wore. "Master fisherman, huh?

We'll see about that." She smacked the hat's brim down, stepped in front of Griffy, and walked haughtily down the dock.

Griffy awkwardly pushed the brim of his camouflage cap back up with his tackle box. The cap carried the "Master Fisherman" insignia, and Griffy wore it proudly whenever he went fishing.

"Hurry it up, Grif," Pike yelled down the dock, waving his identical Master Fisherman cap. Griffy smiled at the sight of it. *Forget Gil. What did she know, anyway?*

About an hour later, it seemed Gil knew more than Griffy had hoped.

"For master fishermen, you two sure are getting skunked," she taunted from her seat at the boat's bow.

Pike grunted unhappily and made a face back at her. Griffy just sulked and stared at the water. He and Pike sat sandwiched side by side on one of the boat's built-in metal benches. Mitch sat in front of them, strategically placed between the boys and Gil, while Uncle Dell ran the motor. Gil, Mitch, and Dell had all caught at least one bass. Pike and Griffy had nothing. Not one tap, and not even a snag.

"This stinks," Pike grumbled.

"No kidding," Griffy agreed sullenly. The largemouth bass with its gaping, translucent mouth and feisty nature, was one of his favorite fish to catch. Everyone's whooping and hollering was really starting to annoy him. Did they really have to yell every time they had a bite?

"I've got another one!" Gil squealed as if reading his mind.

That's just great, Griffy thought, sneering.

Gil battled the largemouth bass on the end of her line. It broke water, showing off its greenish gold body and dark, horizontal stripe as it tried to throw the hook.

"This isn't fair," Pike whined. "How can *she* be catching fish, and we aren't?"

"Get the net! Get the net!" Gil yelled when the fish crashed back down. Griffy sluggishly obeyed and scooped the bass up out of the water.

"That's just a baby," Pike grunted. "Not even worth the trouble."

"Well, at least I got one in the boat, which is more than the two of you can say," she huffed.

"Whatever," Pike and Griffy shot back in unison. Then the two boys sat in silence.

"Oh, quit your moping," Uncle Dell ordered. "There's a bass right up under that pontoon raft. Cast up there and get it." As he said this, Uncle Dell used the trolling motor to guide the boat closer to the raft that was anchored in the bay for swimmers and sunbathers.

Griffy cast out. His bright blue surface lure landed just to the left of the raft. "Perfect," Uncle Dell said. Pike cast out, and his black and gold jointed lure landed just to the right of it. "Another good shot."

Pike and Griffy reeled in, eagerly working their lures through the water. The hooks came up to the boat and out of the water with no hit, no tap, no nothing. Gil snickered.

The boys shot Dell looks of disappointment and betrayal. "There's nothing under that raft," Griffy said as the trolling boat glided farther and farther down the bay.

"Yeah, nothing. You don't know where the fish are," Pike challenged.

"I don't?" Uncle Dell asked. "Well, let's just see. If you won't catch that fish, I will." He turned the boat around and glided back toward the swim raft. "Let me show you how it's done. First, you cast up under the pontoon." Uncle Dell's lure flew through the air, hit the side of the pontoon, and plopped into the water. "You let the lure sit there a bit." They waited. "OK. He sees it now. So, you take the slack out of the line and give it a little jerk to entice him and get his attention."

Uncle Dell had Griffy, Pike, and Gil's attention, at least. Amused, the three watched Dell closely and listened in silence.

"Now you reel in," Dell instructed as he began to work his lure toward the boat. "He's following it. He's following it," he quietly chanted. "He can't help himself. He can't resist. Now, he bites. You jerk to set the hook, and voilà! You've got a fish."

Griffy rolled his eyes and laughed.

"Good one, Dell," Pike chuckled.

Griffy's face suddenly changed from a look of amusement to one of disbelief as the tip of Dell's fishing pole bent dangerously low to the water. "Hey, he's really got a fish!" he exclaimed.

"Of course I do," Uncle Dell replied confidently.

"No way." Gil stood up for a better look. "Holy chedda' cheese. Griffy, get the net."

"I can't believe you just did that," Mitch laughed. "Who are you? The Babe Ruth of fishing?"

Griffy grabbed the net and pleaded, "Come on, Uncle Dell. How *did* you do that? There's just no way."

Uncle Dell shrugged innocently and grinned ear to ear as he brought in the three-pound bass. "Guess we know who the *real* master fisherman is."

Another hour passed and the sun, although sitting much lower in the sky, still shined brightly across Lost Land Lake. Griffy squinted against it as he cast his pole over and over.

Strange, he thought, looking around. It was nowhere near dark, yet they were the only ones out on the lake. Earlier, fishing boats had dotted the scenery. Now, he saw no others.

Mitch interrupted his thoughts. "We might want to think about heading in," he announced, pointing to the sky behind the boys.

Griffy turned to see a bolt of lightning flash in the far distance. *Strange*, he thought again. The skies over Lost Land Lake itself were clear and blue, no hint of a storm. But off in the distance ...

"Dad, that's nothing," Pike admonished. "It's too far away. Griffy and I want to keep fishing."

"What do you think, Dell?" Mitch asked.

"We'll keep an eye on it. Head in if it gets worse."

Pike smiled and nodded.

"That OK with everybody?" Mitch asked. Griffy nodded enthusiastically. Gil just shrugged her approval.

Twenty minutes later, Griffy still hadn't caught a thing. He rummaged through his tackle box looking for a better lure. He wasn't sure what to try next. Nothing he threw out there was working today. As he continued rummaging, a sudden gust of wind blew his Master Fisherman cap right off his head, but he caught it just in time. Griffy looked over his shoulder and cringed as a bolt of lightning flashed in the sky, striking much closer than the first. Across the lake, he could see whitecaps forming on the water.

He nudged Pike. "We need to go in," he said bluntly and gulped. When Pike paid no attention, Griffy elbowed him. "We need to go in," he repeated as he pointed at the stormy sky.

Everyone turned to look. What was left of the setting sun had disappeared into darkness. As if on cue, the first clap of thunder rang out. That was all it took. "OK, bring everything in," Uncle Dell commanded. "We're heading home."

They all leaped to action, bringing in poles, securing tackle boxes, and hoisting the anchor. Uncle Dell cranked up the motor, and soon the small boat was bouncing and skidding toward Whispering Pines. The growing waves splashed into the boat, soaking its five passengers. Shivering, Griffy sat with his head lowered against the wind, quietly urging the boat forward. His heart skipped a beat when the boat jolted to a sudden stop. He looked up. They hadn't made much progress. He could see Whispering Pines, but it seemed far away.

"What happened?" Mitch asked, uneasy.

"Don't know," Dell answered. "Motor died." He tried to crank it up, but nothing happened. He tried again without success.

Mitch moved to the back of the rocking boat, ousting Pike and Griffy from their seats. He tried cranking the motor himself, but still it wouldn't turn over. "Hurry, hurry," Gil pleaded.

Griffy watched fearfully as the storm moved closer and closer. The water behind them foamed and churned. Lightning flashed in spidery veins. A loud thunderclap boomed, and Griffy saw a sheet of rain drop from the sky a ways off, but moving steadily toward them. Lightning flashed again, spiraling from the sky and hitting the lake water.

Gil, who thought she was too old for a life jacket, sat on a floatation cushion instead. She grabbed the cushion and held it close to her chest. Her long, brown hair blew wildly around her. She looked at Pike and Griffy, who were bundled securely in life vests.

"Give me one of those," Gil ordered, pointing to a plastic bag under Pike and Griffy's seat. Uncle Dell always had enough vests for everyone tucked in the boat; it was the law.

"Here." With unsteady hands, Griffy passed her the life jacket. "But it won't do you any good," he said.

"What do you mean?"

"We're in a metal boat." His voice cracked with fear. "We'll get electrocuted before we drown."

"Yeah," Pike agreed sinisterly. "Fried into crispy critters."

Lightning struck the water again. Gil shuddered and quickly fastened the vest around her. "I don't care," she whimpered. "At least my head will be above water."

Uncle Dell and Mitch still couldn't figure out what was wrong with the motor. To Griffy, it looked hopeless. If they didn't get the motor running very soon, it would be the end for them all. He would be swept away by the churning water to die alone at the bottom of Lost Land Lake. His parents would never see him again. They'd never find his charred, drowned body. Alone—he'd be alone forever.

Pike clutched Griffy's arm, snapping him from his thoughts. "We're going to die!" he screamed, squeezing Griffy's arm hard.

"Hush," his father scolded. "That's not helping."

Mitch took a cautious look behind him. Griffy saw the adult's face furrow with worry, and then Mitch sat down and started oaring the boat.

"Please, Uncle Dell," Griffy desperately pleaded. "Hurry."

"Gas!" he announced sharply. Griffy could see the tension drain from his uncle's body. "We're out of gas, that's all." Dell shook his head as he quickly refilled the tank.

Griffy breathed a huge sigh of relief, feeling comforted when in no time the boat was speeding toward Whispering Pines again. That is, he felt comforted until Pike yelled out, "We're not going to make it. The storm's moving way too fast. We're going to die!"

"Pike, be quiet," his dad ordered.

The sheet of rain loomed just feet behind them now. Griffy tensed again as raindrops pelted the boat one by one. The wind howled. Lightning crackled around them.

"Look," Gil pointed. She clapped excitedly. "I can see the dock!"

Griffy saw it, too. "We made it!" he exclaimed. Pike finally let go of his arm. The two boys high-fived and cheered.

Uncle Dell barely slowed the boat as they approached the dock at Whispering Pines. Mitch jumped onto the platform with rope in hand as Dell cut the motor, and Mitch secured the boat. "Out!" he ordered as he helped hoist the kids out of the rocking metal boat and onto the wooden dock. Rain poured down. Waves crashed over their feet.

"Leave everything but the poles and tackle," Dell instructed as he handed equipment to Mitch. Gil, Griffy, and Pike ran the items into the lodge and then ran back for more.

"Our bass!" Griffy yelled to Dell over the roaring wind. Dell nodded. He retrieved the fish basket, and the five fishermen ran for the last time to the safety of the lodge.

Just as the porch door banged shut behind them, golf-ball-sized hail exploded from the sky. The storm that had chased them across the lake now hit the peninsula with a fury. Within minutes, the power went out, leaving Whispering Pines in darkness.

✳ ✳ ✳ ✳

The next morning, Griffy ran outside, still in his pajamas. *The storm couldn't have been that bad,* he thought excitedly. Nothing could be bad on a beautiful morning like this. The blue sky sparkled with sunshine. From his loft window, Griffy had heard birds chirping happily outside.

But Mother Nature had deceived him. The sky was bright and clear, but the peninsula was a damp, muddy mess. Griffy shivered against the cool air. *The temperature has to be about fifty,* he thought. Then his whole body sagged as he took in the devastation before him. *Great. Cleanup duty, again. Is it ever going to end?*

Tree branches and limbs littered the ground and covered the cabin roofs. A once tall and stately pine had split in half and fallen on Cabin 3. An uprooted spruce blocked the front door of Cabin 7. Griffy found his kayak lodged deep in a cluster of birch trees. One of the carved black bears that welcomed guests to Whispering Pines lay on its side, the sign it once held high ripped from its grip and left dangling. Hail had pounded the peninsula, leaving cars and boats marred and dented. Downed phone, cable, and power lines lay twisted along the road.

Going back into the lodge, a glum Griffy headed for the bathroom. He pulled on the chain dangling from its ceiling light. He pulled again. Nothing. *Great, still no power.* Sighing wearily, he closed the door and tried to aim as best he could in the dark, windowless room.

By late afternoon, Whispering Pines still had no power. Griffy couldn't believe it. In Chicago, he had never been without power for more than a few hours. It had been practically a whole day now. *A whole day!* As he walked into the kitchen, he flipped the light switch without even thinking. Nothing.

"Might as well give it up. Electricity won't be on any time soon," Uncle Dell said from behind the refrigerator door. Griffy jumped, having not realized he was there. Then he grinned guiltily.

"I know, but I can't help it," he admitted. The light switches seemed to call to him. *Turn me on. Turn me on.* Being without power made Griffy very uneasy. He felt cutoff, more alone than usual. He had no way to reach his parents. Cell phones didn't work at Whispering Pines, with or without power. Now, neither did the landline.

"What are we supposed to do without electricity?" Griffy questioned as he absently rubbed the scar on his left arm. "You can't do anything without electricity. Can't use the phone. Can't watch TV or use the VCR or the DVD player. Can't use the computer, the Internet. I can't even charge my iPod. It's like the world has been put on pause." He desperately threw his hands up in the air.

Uncle Dell clapped Griffy on the back and smiled reassuringly. "Can't do most of that stuff here, anyway. We've got generators to power the essentials. We'll be fine. No worries."

Again with the no worries. Griffy sighed. He wasn't comforted. He had learned the night before that generators meant very dim lights, if any. Plus the humming, vibrating machines kept pooping out. "Uh-huh. OK. But what are we going to *do* without power?" he whined.

"Keep cleaning up," Dell answered. "Let's get back at it." He handed Griffy some thawing hamburger and a gallon of ice cream. "The freezer house is up and running on a generator.

51

Transfer everything from here to there, OK?" Hauling food was better than hauling tree branches, so Griffy nodded and got to work.

That evening, Mitch and another man boated over from The Happy Hooker to find the Whispering Pines guests out in force helping Dell and Griffy clean up the grounds. Mitch's companion was Andy Gibson who, Griffy remembered, was the publicity-hungry president of the Chequamegon Lake Association. The boy watched as Andy, chewing on a piece of straw, eyed the property. "No one injured?" Andy asked, twirling the straw back and forth in his mouth.

"No," Dell replied. "Everyone's fine here."

"Good. Good," he nodded. "Don't expect power for a while. It'll likely take days before crews can get in here. Trees down all over."

"Days?" Griffy blurted out.

"That's right. The storm system that moved through was a real whopper. Minong's a mess. Unfortunately, Chequamegon residents aren't priority number one, but I'm workin' on it." He winked at Griffy, who looked helplessly from face to face. No one seemed to think this was a problem. *Are they all nuts?* he wondered.

Andy tried to reassure him. "The power goes out all the time, especially in the winter. It's no big deal."

"No big deal?" Griffy questioned. "Are you kidding? What are we supposed to do without power for days?"

"Well, I've got an answer for you," Mitch chimed in. "We got off easy at The Happy Hooker. Barely touched. So I thought Dell and I would start clearing the road. Maybe get you your power faster?"

Griffy liked that idea. He smiled brightly. But Mitch said, "You, Pike, and Gil can go down to Sleepy Eye and help Danny clean up there." Griffy *didn't* like that idea. He had been hauling tree limbs and brush for hours. Scrapes and cuts covered his arms and legs.

"Danny got hit hard, huh?" Dell asked.

Mitch nodded.

"Well then it's off to Sleepy Eye for you, young man," Uncle Dell announced.

Griffy drifted into a daze. His eyes glassed over. *Not more cleanup duty. Good Gouda. It really is never going to end.*

"Tomorrow," Uncle Dell reassured him, giving Griffy a nudge. Griffy staggered slightly. "First thing tomorrow, OK?" Griffy reluctantly nodded his approval.

"Still worried about the power?" Andy asked with a slight chuckle. Mitch and Dell grinned.

"No," Griffy answered. "I'm worried about my aching body."

FAME AND GLORY, PART II

The storm system that buried Griffy's kayak in the trees wreaked havoc on the Village of Minong. The *Minong Ledger*'s front page screamed one word: "Disaster." The newspaper report listed one devastating event after another. Dozens of trees upended. Homes destroyed. Stores reduced to rubble.

The village's greatest loss, the *Ledger* reported, was the new $1.8 million Minong Natural History Museum. Just opened two weeks earlier, the museum now sat crushed by dozens of cedar and pine logs that the storm's violent winds had picked up from the nearby Lumberjack Bowl, driving them like spears into the museum's roof, windows, and walls. These logs, being stored for the upcoming Lumberjack World Championships, ranged in width from twelve to twenty inches and were up to sixty feet long.

The natural history museum was supposed to be a moneymaking feather in the cap of a community that survived on tourism. It had taken the village five years to finance and build the state-of-the-art facility. It took the storm five minutes to destroy it.

Emmett Potts tucked a copy of the *Ledger* under his arm. He straddled a white pine once destined for the women's logrolling competition as he struggled to maneuver his way through the destroyed museum. His yellow hard hat slipped forward, covering his eyes. *Darn hat.* It was way too big for him. He tried to push it back up but in doing so lost his balance and slid sideways. He thrust one hand out to steady himself, and it ripped across the top of the log, driving a thick splinter into his palm. Emmett bit back a painful cry as he regained his balance. Embarrassed, he looked around suspiciously. Construction workers milled about around him. Crew members yelled orders to one another. Hammering and the hum of machinery filled the air. *No one saw that. Good.*

"Professor Potts."

Emmett jumped at the sound of his name and quickly removed himself from the log. He turned to see Gloria Nordman, the museum's executive director, approaching. She said, "There you are. Thank you for coming."

"Actually, it's Dr. Potts," he corrected her, shaking her hand.

"Quite a mess we've got here." Gloria held her arms out and turned in a half circle. "Wouldn't you say?"

"Yes, quite unfortunate." Emmett tapped the newspaper under his arm.

The woman nodded and motioned for Emmett to follow her. "Come this way, professor." She spoke loudly over the constant noise. "Let's have a seat in here so we can talk." She led him to a small room and shut the door behind them. "For an office, this is best I've got right now," she said with an apologetic grin as she took off her own hard hat and laid it on the makeshift desk. "So now, Professor Potts ..."

Emmett quickly interrupted her. "It's Dr. Potts. Doctor. Potts."

"Yes, right. I'm sorry." She smiled and began again. "I wish some good news would come out of this storm. I really do. But I'm afraid right now I don't have any. You see the work we've got here and, well, quite frankly, we are tapped out. I've been instructed by the board of directors to pull funding on projects that aren't producing. That, unfortunately, includes the Big Crooked Lake site."

"What? I don't understand." Emmett hadn't expected this. Anger and anxiety rose in him. He clenched the sides of his chair. "We are doing very important work at Big Crooked Lake. Very important. We recently uncovered some very promising stoneware. Very promising. I don't understand this. Doesn't the museum carry insurance for such things?"

"Yes. Yes, of course. We've just been hit with too much, too fast. We're still paying for the museum's dedication ceremony and opening gala. That was only a few weeks ago ... now this."

Gloria gave Emmett a helpless there's-nothing-I-can-do shrug. She had stopped talking, obviously waiting for a response from him, but he just sat there staring at her. She adjusted her suit jacket and continued. "We just don't have the money right now to fund your site. Next summer we can look at renewing our support. If the site was producing, it'd be a different story.

The museum is extremely dedicated to advancing research and discovery."

She stopped talking again. Emmett still gave no response.

"Professor Potts?" Her voice cracked slightly. Emmett just sat there, staring. "Professor Potts?" she asked again.

"How much time do I have?" he finally answered.

"Until the end of the month. Professor Potts ..."

"Fine," he stated flatly, cutting her off. Emmett stood up. The anger he had been struggling to suppress rose to the surface. His face turned a blotchy red. Beads of sweat broke out across his forehead. "For the last time," he said bitterly, "it's *Dr.* Potts." A threatening tone filled his voice. "I do suggest you remember that."

Gloria nodded slowly as the two heatedly locked eyes. She was nervously pulling on her suit jacket again, but she never took her eyes off him.

Emmett finally broke the stare. Without another word, he turned and walked out.

SLEEPY EYE

"Why didn't we take *The Lucky 13*?" Pike asked as he and Griffy watched Gil land the small wooden boat on the shore at Sleepy Eye Rentals. They stood at the top of the sloping, sandy driveway already tired from their trek on foot down Peninsula Road. Debris and downed trees had made the half-mile walk much longer and required more effort than the two had expected.

"Dunno," Griffy shrugged. "But I'm wishing we would have."

Spinner had followed them down the road, running in and out of the woods, leaping here and there and over this and that with what seemed like no effort at all. He now sat panting loudly next to the boys.

Gil grinned smugly and waved at them.

"She's such a know-it-all," Pike sneered as he, Griffy, and Spinner continued down to the Sleepy Eye office.

Griffy had to force himself to keep walking. He didn't know how he was going to make it through yet another day on cleanup duty. Muscles and places he hadn't known he had hurt. Sweaty and hot, Griffy sluggishly shuffled along wishing he could sit down somewhere, anywhere. *In front of a big flat-screen TV would be very nice*, he thought just as his foot caught on something that sent him sprawling spread-eagle to the ground.

"Dude," Pike snickered. Then he started to laugh so hard he had to grab his side and bend over to stop. "You should have seen that. One minute you're walking, the next minute: splat."

Stunned by the abrupt fall, Griffy just lay there not moving. Spinner stepped on his back and then nudged him under the arm with his nose.

"Hey, you OK?" Pike asked in between snorts of dying laughter.

Griffy spit out grass and sandy dirt. Spinner's wet, saliva-dripping snout suddenly poked his face. *Yuck.* Griffy pushed the dog away and looked out ground level across the property.

Ropes. A maze of knotted ropes crisscrossed the ground, and he'd tripped on one. They were difficult to see when walking because of all the leaves, pine needles, and branches strewn about by the storm. But at ground level, you couldn't miss them.

"I'm all right," he finally grunted, lifting himself up. "What's with all the ropes?"

"Huh?" Pike questioned. He followed Griffy's gaze. "Oh. Yeah. Weird."

"Not too weird, I hope."

The reply startled Pike and Griffy. They turned quickly to find a young man wearing mirrored aviator sunglasses walking toward them. He had straight, shoulder-length blond hair and was dressed in a hockey jersey and camouflage pants. He followed one of the ropes with his hands.

"These ropes are my best friends." The man smiled. "Now that is weird, I know. But seriously, I couldn't get anywhere without them. Watch out, 'cause they're all over the property. Hate when they just jump up and grab you like that, though." He chuckled. "I should post a warning: 'Beware of Ropes'."

Griffy laughed slightly at that, although the whole situation had left him a little uneasy. He didn't know what to think of this guy.

"So, welcome to Sleepy Eye," the man continued. "You must be Pike and Griffy. Gil must be who I hear walking up the hill there. And this fellow," he bent down to pet Spinner, "well, we've met before, but not by name. I'm Danny Rubedieux. Glad you all came over."

He let one hand go of the rope and extended it toward them. Pike just stood there looking very confused. Griffy hesitated but stepped up and shook it. "That's Spinner," he said as the dog ran down to the lake for a drink of water.

"Oh yeah," Pike abruptly blurted out. "You're blind."

"*Pike*," Gil admonished as she walked up to the scene. She popped her brother lightly in the back of the head. "Sorry, Danny. My brother lacks manners and memory."

Pike shot Gil an annoyed look. "I forgot, all right. I never come down here."

"Not a problem," Danny chuckled. He smiled encouragingly. "Yep, I'm blind. Can't see a darn thing. It's very annoying. I use the ropes to get around. By counting the knots," he grabbed one and shook it, "I can get myself exactly where I want to be."

"Oh." Pike nodded his head thoughtfully. "That's smart." He looked around the property and then asked, "What's it like, you know, being blind?"

"Pike!" Gil admonished again. "Would you stop?"

"What? What's wrong with that? Have you met a blind person before? Huh? Have you?"

"Well, no," Gil admitted.

"OK, then. It's a good question, right?" Pike looked for approval from Griffy, then Danny. "Right?"

Griffy nodded but kept his mouth shut. He didn't want to say the wrong thing. Uncle Dell had neglected to tell him, also, that the owner of Sleepy Eye Rentals was blind. *Too much else on his mind*, Griffy guessed.

"There are no bad questions. Isn't that the saying?" Danny replied. "You can ask anything you like. It's OK with me. But what it's like is a difficult one to answer." He paused, ran a hand through his hair, and then continued. "Every moment of every day is filled with uncertainty. Imagine having to do everything in the dark. And I mean everything. You never really know what's what."

Griffy motioned his head eagerly in agreement. He'd been living in the dark for two days now. "We don't have power," he said hurriedly. "I've had to pee in complete darkness. Don't know if I hit the mark or not. Won't know until the lights come back on."

Gil, obviously embarrassed, lowered her head and shook it side to side. But Danny burst out laughing. "That's exactly it. You've got it."

Griffy loosened up. This guy was all right. He made a face at Gil. "How long have you been blind?" he asked.

"Nine years. But wait. How 'bout I answer all your questions while we work instead of just standing here? I can really use your help down by the docks and lagoon. Sound good?"

Pike nodded his OK until Gil elbowed him in the side and shot him a "duh" look. Out loud, all three said, "OK."

"Great. Let's get to it then."

Sleepy Eye's shallow lagoon, where Danny stored pontoons and small motorboats, was overrun with fallen trees. Bloated dead fish floated about. Griffy grimaced as he scooped up their stiff, gray bodies. Most of them were missing their eyes, and Griffy tried very hard not to look into the hollow, gaping sockets. Dead fish and downed trees weren't the only problems. The storm had stirred up a lot of weeds, driftwood, and algae, all of which seemed to have ended up in the Sleepy Eye lagoon.

As the group worked to clear the water, Danny Rubedieux told his story. In high school, Danny was a cocky, all-star hockey player who'd caught the attention of the Minnesota State Mavericks. The scouts loved him, and he earned a full scholarship to play for the university.

"Man, was I good," he continued. "A real superstar. I ranked third on the Mavericks' all-time list. The best forward around. I had a record of three power play goals, four shorthanded goals, and four game-winning goals. I was hot stuff. I was cocky, arrogant, basically a big jerk. Then the Pittsburgh Penguins came calling."

The Penguins lured Danny away from college during his junior year and signed him to a two-year, entry-level NHL contract. "I was going to *the* NHL. I had made it. I thought nothing could stop me, nothing could touch me. I couldn't wait. I dropped out of college right then."

Danny finished out the year playing for the Penguins' amateur team in the American Hockey League.

"That's when the good went bad. We were playing against the Manitoba Moose. I got in a fight. Guy head checked me. Knocked my helmet off. Not a legal move, you know. That got me fired up, so I pummeled the guy. The ref sent me to the penalty box. I could have put the helmet back on. Should have put it back on. But I didn't. As soon as my two minutes were up, I was out of that box, skating for a goal. It was beautiful. Puck was right there. The rest I really don't remember. I was told I got tripped at the net and fell hard. My head hit the ice and the net's metal base. I was out cold. When I woke up, I was blind."

Gil, Griffy, and Pike gasped. The three kids had stopped working and were just staring at Danny, listening intently to his story. Gil was the first to speak. "I'm sorry," she said meekly. "I didn't know. That's really awful."

"Yes, it was," Danny replied bluntly. "But it got worse. I went from superstar to sad, pathetic guy overnight. The NHL, Minnesota State, my coaches—all my so-called friends just disappeared. I think that was the worse part, being abandoned. Being alone. No one wanted to hang with the former superstar jerk turned blind guy."

"What about your family?" Griffy asked. "Where were they?" He felt a sad sort of camaraderie forming with this man. Danny's story about being alone really hit home.

"It was just my mom and me. She died a while back. I inherited this place from my granddad. Been running it a couple years now."

"So, you're all alone?" Griffy asked, a hint of sadness in his voice.

"I have help come in a couple times a month, but basically, yes."

"Wow," was all Pike could find to say. A somber silence fell over the group.

"OK, OK, I really know how to kill a party, huh?" Danny flashed a big smile. "The story's a downer, I know. But I'm over it all, really. And good did come from it. I'm not so much of a jerk anymore. I'm kind of a cool guy, right?"

He gave another big smile but got no response. "Right?"

The kids eagerly agreed this time.

"Well gee, thanks," Danny replied sarcastically. "Doesn't mean so much if I have to beg for it." With that, Danny finally got the three kids to lighten up and laugh a little.

"So, moral of my story is to keep your ego in check. Be humble. Arrogance is not a good thing. Got it?"

"Got it," Pike nodded. He looked out along the shoreline. "You know something else that's not a good thing? Your docks. Looks like all three are about ready to collapse."

"What?" Danny questioned sharply.

"Yeah," Griffy agreed. "They're not looking so good."

"That's just great. Dang storm." Danny sighed and shook his head heavily. "Business has not been that great, kids. Here's another downer from Danny: I'm broke. This storm could pull me under. Then what?" The man sat down where he stood on the edge of the water, defeated.

Griffy exchanged a confused, concerned look with Pike. They could tell that the collapsing docks had nothing to do with storm damage. Sleepy Eye Rentals was already an eyesore, run down and falling apart.

"Don't worry," Griffy assured Danny. He wasn't about to abandon this guy. "We'll get it fixed." He looked to Pike and Gil. "Right?"

"Right," they agreed.

"We can fix it and a lot of other stuff around here," Pike continued. "No problem."

"And we can help you drum up some business," Gil eagerly added. "We'll tell everyone at The Happy Hooker and at Whispering Pines to check out Sleepy Eye."

The next afternoon, Pike, Gil, and Griffy returned to Sleepy Eye ready to work. While the others repaired the docks, Griffy continued cleaning up the lagoon. He worked his way to the far edge where the lagoon met the main body of Lost Land Lake. Shallow Pass was right around the bend.

Griffy, still in those darn muck boots, waded near the bank raking up weeds and picking up driftwood. Suddenly a loud rustling in the woods beyond caught him off guard. He stopped dead in his tracks. The woods surrounded the lagoon, except for the section near Sleepy Eye that Danny kept clear. Facing the woods, Griffy stood motionless, listening. The rustling began again, and he heard branches cracking. Something was moving out there. He gripped the rake tighter.

Before he could do anything, Spinner bolted out of the woods and nearly knocked him over.

"Spinner!" he cried out in relief. "You scared me to death. Crazy dog."

Spinner bounced happily through the lagoon, carrying an odd looking piece of driftwood in his mouth. It looked to be about a foot long with a splintered fork at one end and a rounded bulb at the other. "Hey, whatcha got there?" Griffy clapped and called for the dog to come, but instead he ran up on shore away from Griffy. "Come on, Spinner. Let me see." Griffy walked over to the dog and bent down to take the driftwood. Spinner hunkered down and growled so fiercely that Griffy jumped back and stared in shock at the dog. Spinner had never growled like that at him before.

"I just want to see it. I'm not going to take it from you," he said soothingly as he reached out again. Spinner growled, this time deep and low in his throat. Griffy pulled back. He knew that animals could sense fear. He also knew it was important for Spinner to remember who was boss. He didn't think the dog would bite him. Spinner just really wanted that piece of driftwood. Griffy pulled himself together. He looked sternly at the dog and then ordered in a forceful voice, "Drop it."

Still hunkered down with the driftwood clenched in his mouth, Spinner looked quizzically at Griffy. His two white, bushy eyebrows went up, then down, then up again. Griffy locked his eyes on Spinner. "Drop it," he ordered again.

Just as Griffy reached for the driftwood one more time, the woods behind him rustled loudly. He turned and froze with fear when he saw what was making the noise. A large black bear lumbered through the woods just feet away. Spinner finally dropped the driftwood; he ran in front of Griffy, growling and barking fiercely at the bear.

"Don't move," Danny shouted in the distance. Griffy moved only his eyes to watch Danny grab a rope and run up the hill. Within seconds, an air horn sounded.

The bear took off. Spinner charged after him.

"No! Spinner, come back!" Griffy yelled. Then, without even thinking, he ran into the woods after the dog.

66

"Grif!" Pike bellowed from the dock. "Get back here!" The air horn continued to sound. Pike, who was taller, thinner, and faster than Griffy, quickly caught up with him and practically tackled him in the woods.

"Good Gouda. What're you thinking? You don't chase bears."

"We have to get Spinner," Griffy pleaded.

A painful yelp suddenly filled the air and drew the boys' attention out to Shallow Pass. There, two bears hungrily feasted on dead fish. A third bear bolted out of the woods and splashed into the water. Spinner was nowhere to be seen.

Griffy's stomach twisted and turned. "He was protecting me. Now he's hurt. We've got to find him."

The sound of the air horn grew steadily closer as Danny, with Gil as his guide, made his way through the woods. Both he and Gil carried hockey sticks.

"Where are they? Where are they?" Danny shouted in panic.

"They're OK. I see them, I see them," Gil assured. Griffy could hear the relief in her voice.

"Don't ever do that again," Danny harshly scolded when he and Gil finally caught up with the boys. "How many bears?"

"Three," Griffy said. His body was shaking from the inside out. "They're in Shallow Pass."

"All of you stay put," Danny ordered. Using the hockey stick to guide his way, he moved steadily toward the water. He sounded the air horn over and over.

"It's working," Gil shouted. "They're leaving." With that she ran up to Danny to help him back.

"Spinner," Griffy urged. "We have to find Spinner."

"He's hurt, or worse," Pike explained.

Danny hesitated, and then he reluctantly nodded. "OK. Gil, stay with me. Keep an eye on the pass, and keep the boys in sight. You two go find the dog. Quickly."

It didn't take the boys long to locate Spinner. The dog lay whimpering on the shore of Shallow Pass. The boys quickly ran to his side.

Blood covered the dog's back legs. "Looks like he's been clawed," Pike said. "Not too bad, I think. Poor guy."

"It's OK, Spinner. It's OK." Griffy said as he carefully picked the dog up. Spinner whimpered softly. Pike gently petted his head as they made their way back to Gil and Danny.

"I think we will need Dell for this one," Danny said when he heard the details of Spinner's injuries. "Gil, can you run ahead and get him?"

Gil didn't give an answer; she just took off running toward *The Lucky 13*.

The piece of driftwood Spinner had wanted so badly caught Griffy's eye as they walked past the lagoon toward Sleepy Eye. "Pike, grab that," he said, motioning toward the object. "That's Spinner's. He's going to want it."

"Sure thing," Pike said. "Whatever our hero wants, our hero gets."

SPINNER

Spinner lay serenely in a patch of sunlight on the lodge's screened porch, his beloved piece of driftwood securely positioned under his front paws. Pike and Griffy stood nearby.

"Do you think he needs a pillow?" Griffy asked. The wood plank floor didn't look that comfortable.

"Naw," Pike answered. "He seems peaceful."

Griffy nodded.

"Crazy dog, chasing after bears," Pike scolded in a hushed voice. He shook his head.

"And the way he carried on about that piece of driftwood, barking and snarling like that, you'd think it was a bone or something," Griffy added. But he agreed. *Crazy, brave dog.*

Spinner had done battle with a bear and had the scars and mangled looks to prove it. The poor dog was shaved bald in patches so the vet could stitch up his gashes. The bear had also fractured his back leg, which was now in a cast. Griffy sighed in pity as he continued staring at Spinner.

Then a puzzled look slowly surfaced on his face. *Wait a minute.* He quietly knelt down next to the dog. "It *is* a bone," Griffy whispered.

"What?" Pike asked, moving closer.

Griffy looked up at him. "It's a bone. A fossilized bone." He very carefully removed the object from under Spinner's paws and held it up for Pike to see. "It looks like a femur."

"A what-ur?" Pike chuckled.

Griffy rolled his eyes. "A femur. You know, a leg bone." Griffy tapped his thigh. "And from a very large animal."

Pike shrugged. "So?"

"So," Griffy answered, his voice edged with impatience, "it could be old. Very old. From the Ice Age, even. It looks just like the fossilized bones I studied at the Field Museum in Chicago." Griffy stood up and examined the bone from every angle. "I can't believe I didn't see it before." He shook his head in amazement, silently scolding himself.

"The Ice Age? Yeah, right," Pike scoffed. "Nothing could survive the Ice Age."

"And why not?" Gil asked as she boldly entered the porch area. The door banged shut behind her. Spinner jerked awake at the noise.

"Shhh," Pike and Griffy scolded in unison, pointing at the dog.

Gil cringed. "Sorry."

Spinner's head shot up. He looked around for a moment but then dropped his head back down and slept again. The three kids moved away from the dog and quietly huddled in a corner.

"Um, it was the Ice Age, as in ice—*everywhere*," Pike finally replied.

"Um," Gil mocked, "and it lasted for thousands and thousands of years. The entire planet wasn't covered in ice. Anyway, the glaciers retreated as the earth warmed. Animals and people existed. You *do* go to school, don't you?"

"Yes," Pike fired back. Then he shamefully added, "But I don't always pay attention."

"What did you think, the planet was one big skating rink?" Gil smirked. "Yeah, everyone just skated around licking icebergs."

"Shut up," Pike ordered. "I wasn't thinking, all right?"

"Obviously. Maybe you should try paying attention in class. You might learn something useful."

Pike scowled. "OK, Mom," he replied sarcastically.

Griffy barely heard their bickering. He was too lost in his own thoughts. This bone could be the answer to Danny's problems. An animal bone from the Ice Age would be a major find. Griffy was sure universities and museums would jump at the chance to excavate Danny's lagoon. And if the bone dated back ten thousand years or more … Griffy's eyes glazed over at the thought. Butterflies danced in his stomach.

"We've got to get this bone radiocarbon dated," he said urgently, excitement filling his voice. "Find out exactly how old it is." Pike and Gil stopped arguing and listened. "This could mean a lot of money for Danny—and publicity, a lot of publicity for Sleepy Eye and Lost Land Lake. It could be a huge archaeological find." He lifted his arms up wide in the air. "Huge! Archaeologists, zoologists, biologists, and who knows who else would want to study it."

"So, how do we do that? You know, get it radio-whatever dated?" Pike asked. His eyes sparkled with enthusiasm.

"We take it to a museum or university and convince them to analyze it."

Pike's eyes quickly dulled. "Oh, is *that* all? OK, so again, how we gonna do that?"

A knowing smile filled Gil's face. "Shouldn't be a problem," she stated.

"How do you figure that?" Pike demanded. "We're just going to walk into a museum and say, 'Here's a bone our dog found. Go study it.'?"

"No, silly. There's a site being excavated right now near Big Crooked Lake. I read about it in the newspaper. I think the group is from the University of Wisconsin. We could take the bone there." Gil lifted the bone from Griffy's hands and eyed it curiously. "I could take you over in the cart."

"Cool!" Griffy exclaimed. As far as he was concerned, Uncle Dell's Army green, bumper sticker-covered golf cart was the only way to travel.

"Wait a minute," Pike interjected. He stepped in front of Gil, pushing her back a step, and spoke directly to Griffy. "Listen. We don't need *her* to take us anywhere. This is our find, not hers. Dell will do it, or my Dad."

"Not likely," the older girl said.

"Hey, will you stay out of this?" Pike glanced over his shoulder and shot his sister an angry look.

"No, I won't," she stated matter-of-factly. "This is too cool. And anyway, the reason I came in here is to tell you that Peninsula Road is blocked. No way in, no way out."

"What?" Griffy blurted out. "You mean we have no power, *and* we're trapped?" The butterflies in his stomach quickly died.

"Sort of. You know Mossy Rock?"

Griffy nodded that he did. It was more of a large boulder than a rock.

"Well, crews were out clearing the road. They removed a fallen tree not realizing it was holding another, half-fallen one in place. When that one fell completely, its root system popped up and catapulted Mossy Rock into the middle of Peninsula Road. The cart will barely squeeze by. Forget an SUV or truck."

"Doesn't mean Da …" Pike started, but Gil quickly cut him off.

"Dad and Dell are too busy figuring out how to get vacationers in here. Luckily, those who needed to get out did. But Dell can't afford a week's worth of cancellations. And Mom's too busy at The Happy Hooker. No one has time for this right now," she waved the bone in front of Pike's face, "but me."

"Hey, be careful with that!" Griffy cried out, grabbing the bone from Gil. "OK, OK. We're in. Right, Pike?" He didn't care who was offering. He wasn't missing out on a trip to a real archaeology site or a ride in the cart. Both were way too much fun.

Pike sighed miserably. "Yeah," he reluctantly agreed, "we're in. But what about him?" Pike nodded toward Spinner. "He's gonna want that bone when he wakes up."

Griffy quickly disappeared into the lodge. He reappeared moments later carrying a very large meat bone. Pike's eyes widened at the sight of it. Griffy smiled broadly. "A gift from Danny. Should do the trick, I think."

Pike nodded. "Definitely."

FAME AND GLORY, PART III

Emmett Potts sat on the ground, hands resting on his knees as he watched his students scurry about the dig site at Big Crooked Lake. The air was tense, the activity hectic. Emmett was in a foul mood. The scowl covering his face had been there for days. The Minong Natural History Museum's funding was quickly running out, and still nothing of significance had been unearthed. A couple students cautiously walked by darting fearful looks at him as they passed. *Good*, he thought. *Stay away. Stay far away.*

All was lost. Emmett knew it. He drifted into deep thought as he rubbed his neatly trimmed beard back and forth. *What to do? What to do? What to do?*

He didn't know. All he knew was that no one was going to force him into retirement. He wasn't going to let his career end like this. Never! When he goes, it would be on a wave of accolades and accomplishments. Emmett removed a handkerchief from the pocket of his khaki work pants, dabbed his sweaty face with it, and then tied it around his neck. He sighed heavily. *What to do? What to do?*

"Potts?" A hesitant voice spoke out. It was his good-for-nothing assistant. The man didn't know the meaning of respect. There was never a title—no "doctor," no "professor," just "Potts."

"What?" Emmett barked tersely.

The assistant took a step back. "There are some kids here. I thought you might want to meet with them."

"What!" Emmett barked again, and then he began to rant. "You bother me for some kids? Kids! Why on earth would I want to meet with kids now, when everything is falling apart? Kids! Do I look like I'm in the mood to talk with kids?"

Emmett saw the look on his assistant's face. It was one of loathing. All he needed right now was this good-for-nothing to file a bad report with the university. Then the face stiffened as if his assistant had just rediscovered his backbone. "I thought it might be good public relations in light of the situation," he sternly lectured. "You didn't leave a very positive impression on Gloria Nordman. The university wants to stay on good terms with the natural history museum and the people of Minong."

"Yes," Emmett hurriedly agreed. "Quite right. Good idea. Very good." He nodded approvingly and slowly stood up, waving his brimmed straw hat at a squadron of attacking insects. He pointed the hat forward. "Bring them to my tent."

Emmett went there himself. He was sitting behind his desk when the tent flap opened and three kids walked in: a girl and two boys. They had something wrapped up in newspaper and looked eager, even excited. *Great.* Emmett forced a smile. "Good day. I'm

Dr. Emmett Potts. What can I do for you?" He rested his hands in his lap and impatiently tapped one against the other. *Let's see how quick we can make this.* He raised his eyebrows, waiting.

The shorter of the two boys spoke up. "We wanted you to take a look at this. We think it's a fossilized bone. I've studied them at the Field Museum—in Chicago." The boy unwrapped the object and held it out.

Immediately Emmett's heart jumped. It *was* a fossilized bone. *Stay calm,* he instructed himself. He turned it over and over, examining it from every angle. *The bone has butchering marks! That means tools. Which means people, possibly Paleo-Indians.* He'd need to have it radiocarbon dated, but …

"Where did you get this?" he asked, keeping his voice monotone, disinterested.

"Our dog found it. Over at Lost Land Lake," the taller boy answered.

"Hmmm. Interesting, interesting." Emmett nodded his head. "Whereabouts exactly?"

The small boy: "In the lagoon at Sleepy Eye Rentals."

"In the water?" Emmett asked with astonishment. "You found it in the water?" He had never thought to excavate the lake bottom. *Interesting, indeed.* The storm must have stirred up the lake sediment and brought this bone—and perhaps others—to the surface.

The girl was talking now. "We thought maybe you could carbon date it. Right, Griffy?" The smaller boy nodded enthusiastically.

Emmett ignored the request. "Have you showed this to anyone else? My assistant, perhaps?"

"No. He gave us a site tour, but we waited to show it to you," the boy called Griffy responded.

Emmett's composure faltered. "Oh, good," he chirped happily. "Very good."

The girl's eyes narrowed, and Emmett knew immediately that he had sounded entirely too relieved by the boy's answer. He quickly recovered, stating flatly, "Because this is just a piece of driftwood. Nothing more."

The eager, excited looks left the kids' faces. *That's what I want to see.* He almost smiled but instead forced a small frown. "Ah, no need for those long faces. It was an easy mistake." He stood up and ushered them out of the tent. "I need to get back to work now. We're very busy here, on the verge of a breakthrough find. Need to get back at it. Always a pleasure meeting young archaeologists like yourselves."

He patted the smaller boy on the back and was about to close the tent flap behind them when the taller boy turned around and held out his hand. Emmett just stared at him.

"The driftwood," tall boy stated. "We need that back."

"Yeah," short boy agreed. "Our dog really loves it."

Emmett hesitated. He looked at the bone in his hand, not wanting to give it up.

This time the girl held out her hand. "It's just a piece of driftwood."

"Yes, of course," Emmett replied quickly, and he handed over the bone.

As the tent flap closed behind the three kids, a sly look filled Emmett's face.

All is not lost, he thought. *No, not at all.*

OH, WHAT A FIND

Almost a week passed after Gil, Pike, and Griffy visited the dig site at Big Crooked Lake. The outing had sent Griffy into a state of depression. Up in the loft, he lay on his stomach stretched out across his bed. He didn't want to do anything. And why should he? Nothing was going his way. The power was still out, Mossy Rock still blocked Peninsula Road, and he had to live with the embarrassment of mistaking a piece of driftwood for an ancient bone. He still couldn't believe he had given a piece of *driftwood* to a real archaeologist. *What an idiot I am.*

"Are you seriously going to just lie up here for the rest of the day?"

Pike poked his head into the loft through the ladder's opening in the floor. Griffy watched, but didn't move, as Pike climbed farther up the ladder and hoisted himself onto the floor. He sat with his feet dangling into the hallway below. "Come on. Snap out of it already. Geez."

Griffy didn't respond.

"I hear they are going to dynamite Mossy Rock. The road is too narrow for any heavy-duty cranes to get down, so they're going to blow it up. Cool, huh? Wanna go check it out?"

Griffy still didn't respond.

"We could go try to catch Big Blue. You haven't done that yet."

Griffy really wanted to catch Big Blue. Sunken Island Resort on the far side of the lake kept the giant bluegill almost as a pet. For kids, it was a big attraction. The fish weighed in larger than the world record holder, but no one kept or killed the fish. It was a silent pact among fishermen at Lost Land Lake—Big Blue was strictly catch and release. But for Griffy, today was not the day. He didn't respond.

"Come on," Pike whined in exasperation. "Do you know how many times *I* mess up? It's no big deal. Move on."

"Hey up there," came a shout from the base of the ladder.

Pike looked down. "Great. It's you."

"Move. I'm coming up," Gil announced.

Pike scooted himself farther into the room as his sister climbed the ladder. She plopped a copy of the *Minong Ledger* onto the floor as she pulled herself into the loft. "You're going to want to see this," she said, taking the paper over and sitting on the bed next to Griffy. "Look."

Gil unfolded the newspaper and pointed to a front-page headline: "Ancient bone unearthed at Big Crooked Lake." The deck head read: "Discovery saves site, museum renews funding."

Griffy bolted upright and grabbed the paper, and at the same time the bed shook as Pike pounced on it. Soon Pike was reading over his shoulder. The article said that Dr. Potts had found a scapula, or shoulder blade, of what he believed to be an ancient elk, dating possibly to 8,000 BC. The evidence of wounding marks on the bone was particularly exciting, Potts was quoted as saying, as it linked the animal to primitive hunters that had lived in the area during the end of the Ice Age. The bone was on its way to be radiocarbon dated at the University of Wisconsin. The article heralded the bone as possibly the earliest artifact of its kind to be found in the state of Wisconsin. All involved eagerly awaited the test results to confirm the finding.

"Seems kind of an odd coincidence, don't you think?" Gil asked.

"It sure does," Pike agreed.

Griffy looked quizzical. "What do you mean?"

"We find a bone. He finds a bone," Pike replied.

"We found a piece of driftwood, not a bone."

"Says who?" Gil shot back. "Dr. Potts? I didn't like that man one bit. Besides, he was way too happy to hear we hadn't shown the 'driftwood' to anyone but him. *Way* too happy."

Pike nodded his head in agreement. "The man was shifty."

"Shifty? What are you saying?"

Gil stared pointedly at Griffy. "I'm saying he lied."

"No way. Not possible. He's an archaeologist. They search for the truth. He wouldn't lie about a find."

"Wouldn't he?" she questioned sharply. "The article says the museum was days away from pulling his funding. Just days away. Then we showed up."

"Yeah, but …"

"Griffy, you were positive that was a fossilized bone. Positive," Pike encouraged.

"I know, but …"

Gil interrupted, "But nothing. It's a bone, end of discussion. And where is it, anyway?"

"I think I left it on the porch."

"Well, let's go get it," Pike announced, jumping off the bed.

Down on the porch, Spinner lay in his favorite spot, sunning himself and chewing on the cast covering his back leg. "Stop that, Spinner," Griffy scolded.

The dog looked up, raised his bushy eyebrows, and then went back to chewing.

"The vet said that cast has to stay on for at least another week," Griffy explained. "The rate he's going, he'll have it chewed off by tomorrow."

"I might have something to distract him," Pike said. "Wait a minute."

He sorted through the large cargo pockets on his shorts, extracting several miscellaneous items before a perplexed look filled his face. "What's this?" he questioned as he pulled out a frog—a live, not very happy frog. It immediately jumped out of his hands. Spinner jumped, too, and hobbled after it, chasing it as best he could, barking enthusiastically.

Pike shrugged. "That's not what I was looking for, but it did the trick."

"You had a frog in your pocket?" Gil shook her head. "Unbelievable."

Griffy snickered. "How long had he been in there?"

"Just since this morning. I forgot about him."

"Well gee, that explains it," Gil said, rolling her eyes.

Pike started to refill his pockets. "Hold up," Griffy ordered, grabbing his friend by the arm. "What's that?" He pointed to a stone object lying among the clutter.

"That? That's just an arrowhead. I'm going to add it to my collection."

Griffy picked it up. "Oh, wow. That's no arrowhead. That's a Clovis point!"

Pike took a closer look. "What do you mean, wow?"

Griffy hesitated. *He couldn't be wrong about this, too. He just couldn't be.* In Chicago, he had spent a lot of time at the Field Museum. He was a member, had taken fossil and archaeology classes, gone on the field trips, and attended lectures by anthropologists and archaeologists. He'd done it all. He could understand his mistake about the bone, but not this. *Not this. I'm certain.*

"Paleo-Indians used Clovis points for hunting about ten thousand years ago," he finally explained. "We're talking the Ice Age again. You can tell by the grooves. See the fluted markings?"

The Clovis point was about an inch and a half wide and three inches long. Griffy could picture an ancient Indian in the forest carrying a long staff with the point on the end. He could see the spear flying through the air toward an unsuspecting animal. "Where did you find this?" he asked.

Pike's eyes sparkled, and his voice raised an octave. "In the Sleepy Eye lagoon. I picked it up when we were helping Danny."

Butterflies danced wildly in Griffy's stomach, just like before. The feeling was almost sickening. *I was right all along. We did find a bone! This proves it.* Griffy did a celebratory dance that would best the end zone dance of any NFL football player. Pike joined in.

"Well, that's all the evidence I need," Gil stated smugly as the two boys spastically danced around the porch. "We've got a

fossilized bone and a Clovis point, both from the same lagoon."
She grabbed Pike and Griffy by the arms, forcing them to stop
and pay attention. "Meanwhile, a certain archaeologist in a
do-or-die situation has discovered a bone of his own. I think
someone has been raiding our lagoon."

In his excitement, Griffy hadn't thought about the possibility
of an archaeological theft. Two discoveries so similar ... he had
to admit it was a very strange coincidence.

"But how?" he asked. "The road's blocked." With all the
equipment and crews being brought in, nothing could get by
Mossy Rock now. Not even the cart.

A knowing smile expanded on Pike's face. "I think I know
exactly how."

EVIDENCE

Pike's bedroom was the coolest Griffy had ever seen. It could be a museum in itself, he thought. The room didn't have a single inch of free wall or shelf space. A spiky blowfish "swam" suspended from the ceiling. A hornet's nest, complete with tree branches, was mounted in one corner. An old wooden airplane propeller was tacked on the wall. Next to it rested an antique hunting bow and quiver of arrows. On shelves, geodes, crystals, and crinoid stems lay scattered among model jet fighters, miscellaneous deer antlers, and an array of old glass bottles. A pair of ancient snowshoes hung crisscrossed on the ceiling above Pike's bed. Everywhere Griffy looked, something extremely cool caught his eye.

Pike had headed straight for a yellowing picture on the wall when they'd entered the room. He took it down and brought it over to Griffy. The two sat on the corner of the bed huddled around it.

"This is that map of Lost Land Lake I told you about—the one from the flea market. See Big Crooked Creek here." Pike pointed to it. On the map, it actually looked like a creek. "It forks a few times but always comes together again, see? When we were kayaking, we went this way. But if you go this way, it takes you straight to Big Crooked Lake. That's got to be how Potts got in."

Griffy studied the map. It made sense. If Potts hadn't gotten to Lost Land Lake by land, it had to have been by water. What didn't make sense was …

He shot Pike a quizzical look. "What do you mean 'we went this way?' How many ways can you go?"

"Several. Like I said, the creek forks a lot. Some of those forks have overflowed and merged into ponds now. But this way is by far the fastest, easiest route. To the lake, anyway."

"You mean we didn't *have* to go up and over that beaver dam? We could have gone a different, easier way?"

"Well, yeah." Pike smiled mischievously. "But those ways aren't as fun."

Griffy could have wrung Pike's neck just then. "Oh, yeah. Getting stuck and attacked by a crawdad was fun. Heaps and loads of it."

Pike nodded playfully. "I know." He laughed and elbowed Griffy in the side.

"I'm never following you again. Forget it."

"Whatever you say," Pike teased. "But you know you will."

Movement in the doorway caught Griffy's eye. It was Gil. "So are you convinced?" she asked.

"Kind of," he replied. He was still having a difficult time believing an archaeologist would make up a find or steal someone else's. That went against everything archaeologists stood for. "It does all make sense. But I still don't know."

"Well, Mom just told me that Dad and Dell are over at Sleepy Eye right now renting pontoons. Let's take *The Lucky 13* over there. It's time to tell someone else what we've found."

Griffy reluctantly nodded his OK. If they were wrong ... well, he really didn't think he could take the embarrassment again.

"You know me," Pike said. "I'm in."

"Good. Let's go."

At Sleepy Eye, Mitch and Dell were down at the docks readying pontoon boats. They filled spare gas tanks, gathered life jackets, swept out debris, and wiped down seats while Danny gave instructions on operating the boats. Some of them were a little touchy from their age and disrepair.

The three kids stood on the dock as Danny fired up an engine. "This one you've got to jiggle the key in the ignition a few times before you turn 'er on. Then she'll turn over just fine. Otherwise, not a chance."

Griffy could see three pontoons out and ready to go. "Uncle Dell, are you renting all of these?" he asked.

"Yep," Dell nodded, still busy at work. "With the road blocked, we need some way to get people in on Saturday. Mitch is letting our guests park at The Happy Hooker. Then we'll load 'em up and ferry 'em over."

"Saturday?" Pike questioned. "Aren't they blowing up Mossy Rock today?"

"Thought so, too," Uncle Dell replied. "Now they're waiting until Monday." The man stopped what he was doing and looked at Griffy, Pike, and Gil. "Glad you kids are here. I need you to stay in the lodge for a while. Keep an eye on things, see if anyone needs anything."

"Sure." Griffy shrugged his OK. "But we came to show you something. Look what we found." He excitedly held up both the bone and the Clovis point.

Dell gave the artifacts a quick glance. "That's good."

"It's a Clovis point," Griffy explained.

"And a fossilized bone," Pike continued.

"We found them in Danny's lagoon," Gil finished.

"Uh-huh. That's great," Uncle Dell said as he tried starting the pontoon motor on his own. "Get on over to the lodge now. We've got a lot to do here."

"But Uncle Dell, these are ancient artifacts," Griffy pleaded. "They date back to the Ice Age. And they were in Danny's lagoon!"

"More importantly," Gil said. "We think that archaeologist—you know, that Dr. Potts—has been stealing *his* artifacts right out of Danny's lagoon."

"Gil!" her father scolded. "Come on, now. That imagination of yours is going to get you in nothing but trouble. Enough, OK?"

Gil hung her head and stayed quiet. Mitch moved up to Griffy and examined the Clovis point. "That's a really nice arrowhead. A very good find." He smiled encouragingly. "But it's going to have to wait. We'll look at it later, OK? We've got a lot to deal with right now."

"Darn right," Uncle Dell agreed. "We've got getting folks in figured out, but we've got to get them out, too. Can't believe those county workers." Dell shook his head in disgust. "Monday! They want to wait until Monday to clear the road. I've got guests who need to leave Friday, and I assume they'll want to take their cars with them. That gives me two days to figure something out. Two days! You don't happen to have a barge stored around here somewhere, do you, Danny?"

Danny frowned and shook his head no.

"The old dump!" Pike blurted out. "What about the old dump? The entrance and exit curve past where Mossy Rock is, I'm sure of it."

Uncle Dell thought for a moment and then slowly nodded his head. "Yes, I think you're right. Good, Pike. Mighty good." He smiled. "The road is gated and locked, but we should be able to get the keys from the county, given the circumstances."

"Road's got to be in bad shape, really overgrown," Mitch said. "How bad, Pike? Do you remember?"

"I haven't been down there yet this summer. It'll probably need some clearing, but an SUV or truck should manage no problem."

"Hallelujah!" Uncle Dell exclaimed with relief. He beamed at the three kids and then turned to Griffy. Nodding at the objects Griffy held, he promised, "We'll take a hard look at those on Sunday when all this is behind us."

Griffy solemnly nodded back. He was used to being dismissed by busy adults.

"Now, let's get the pontoons set up and get over to the dump," Dell instructed.

Danny stood up. "Count me in," he said eagerly. "These kids have really helped me out. I want to return the favor. I might be blind, but I'm strong."

Uncle Dell clapped Danny on the back. "You're in. Wait here, and we'll pick you up when we come back for the third pontoon."

* * * *

"So now what?" Griffy asked as Mitch and Dell pulled away from the dock and out into the open waters of Lost Land Lake. He stared at the artifacts in his hands. He understood that with Uncle Dell, guests had to come first, especially with a problem like this one. But that didn't keep it from feeling like there was a heavy rock in the pit of his stomach now.

No one said a word at first, but then Pike shrugged in defeat. "I guess we go back to the lodge like Dell said and wait until Sunday."

"No, we don't," Gil countered. "First, we go to the lagoon. Look for evidence."

Danny chuckled. Griffy was stunned to hear that mocking tone from Danny. Saddened, he lowered his head. Pike and Gil fell silent, as well. Danny obviously sensed their hurt, as he said, "Sorry. Sorry." He sighed and rubbed his face. "OK, let me have a look at those artifacts. One at a time, please." He held out his hands.

Griffy gave him the Clovis point first, then the leg bone. Danny carefully explored each of them with his hands. When he finished, he bit his lower lip skeptically. "So, you found these in my lagoon, and you think they are from the Ice Age?"

"Yes," Griffy answered. "They could be. If they are ..."

"There'd be a lot of money in it for you," Pike quickly interjected. "Right, Grif?"

"Yep. You'd be paid for the excavation rights."

"By museums and universities," Gil added.

"Really? They'd pay, huh? To dig up my land."

"Yes," Gil continued. "If Potts doesn't clean you out first."

Danny was taken aback, not only by the kids' plan, but also by their enthusiasm to help him out. He smiled slightly. "All right, you've got me. We've got some time before Mitch and Dell return for the other boat, so let's go look for that evidence."

The Sleepy Eye lagoon, too narrow to be called a cove, cut into the peninsula in a rectangular shape. From the lake, it looked more like a secret tunnel, its entrance partially hidden by overhanging trees, grasses, and lily pads. It was just wide enough to navigate two boats through side by side. Today, Danny had three small aluminum fishing boats anchored there.

"What exactly are we looking for?" Danny asked as Griffy and Pike removed their socks and shoes. The two waded along the lagoon's rocky shore. Gil moved into the surrounding woods.

"Not really sure," Pike answered. "Signs of digging. Tools. Maybe a flashlight."

"Yeah," Gil said. "Potts has got to be coming late at night or early in the morning when not a lot of fishermen are out. Maybe he forgot something."

"Have you heard any unusual noises?" Griffy asked.

"No," Danny said, "not really." He paused. "You know, now that I think about it, I have heard more activity down here lately. In the morning around four-thirty, five o'clock. I just figured it was bears."

Gil poked her head out of the woods. "I'm not seeing anything back here."

"Nothing here, either," Pike said.

Griffy waded farther out, looking carefully around the boats. If Potts was really sneaky, he'd have tied a minnow bucket to one of the boats to hide tools in. Or he could …

"Ow!" Griffy cried out as something sharp and pointy pierced the arch of his foot. He instinctively jerked his foot out of the water. Balancing on one leg, he grabbed his ankle to examine the injury. *No blood, good. But that really hurt.* To get a better look, he pulled the sole of his foot closer to his face, but he wobbled and fell backward. As he crashed into the Sleepy Eye lagoon, something sharp stabbed him in the butt, then in the back. "Ow!" he cried out again.

Pike ran over. "What? What is it?" He gave Griffy a hand and hoisted him up out of the water.

"I dunno. I stepped on some …"

"Holy chedda' cheese!" Pike exclaimed as he looked over Griffy's shoulder. Pike quickly shoved him out of the way.

"Hey, watch it!" Griffy turned around to see Pike examining a pointy piece of driftwood sticking up out of the water.

"Whatcha got?" Gil asked, emerging from the woods.

"Yeah," Danny said impatiently. "Holy chedda' cheese what?"

"It's nothing." Griffy waved off their pleas, pointing to the object sticking out of the shallow water. "I just fell on a piece of driftwood, here."

Gil saw and nodded, obviously disappointed.

But Pike snickered, a knowing smile upon his face. "Guys, that's no piece of driftwood." He had crouched down over the object. "I don't know much about femurs or the Ice Age, but I know elk antlers when I see elk antlers. And that's an elk antler."

"What?" Griffy exclaimed. This time it was he who pushed Pike out of the way.

Pike caught his balance, stood up, and carefully pulled the antler from the lagoon's sandy bottom. "Yup, it's one antler.

Look. Six points. These likely came from an elk with a twelve-point rack. A huge one."

"Sweet Brie. How cool is that?" Gil gushed. She kicked off her sandals and splashed into the water for a better look.

"If you're looking for evidence, I'd say you just found it," Danny said. "Seriously, how many ancient elks can be out there?"

Griffy couldn't believe it. He just stood there in a daze staring at the antler. It was too good to be true. A fossilized femur, a Clovis point, and now a fossilized elk antler—all found in the same lagoon. *Wow.* Danny was right; there was no denying it.

Griffy shook himself from his thoughts and snapped into action. "Everybody out," he ordered.

Gil and Pike looked at him quizzically.

"We've got to preserve the site," he explained as he ushered them out of the lagoon. "Who knows what damage we've done already? And most importantly, we've got to keep Potts out of here."

Gil smiled smugly. "So you finally believe me?"

Griffy nodded. "He's stealing from the lagoon. No doubt about that now. We've got to hold him off."

"Well, I'm in," Danny said. "I'll help any way I can. No one's stealing from me and getting away with it. Not if I can help it."

"But how are we going to hold him off until Sunday?" Gil asked. "That's a long time."

Pike chuckled. His eyes had that sparkle in them again. "Oh, I have a few ideas."

Griffy smiled slyly, too. *This is going to be good.*

FAME AND GLORY, PART IV

Emmett Potts sat at his desk lost in thought, his usually ever-present scowl replaced by a thin, cunning grin. His fingers danced absently along his latest find—a tibia, or shinbone, of what was sure to be known as the Potts Elk. *The Potts Elk.* Oh, how he liked the sound of that. And oh, how he liked the look on Gloria Nordman's face when he'd shown her the scapula bone: pure shock. *That shut her up. Show me the money, Gloria. Yes, show me the money.* He snorted his contempt as his grin widened.

The desk clock caught his eye. *Hmmm.* It was later than he had thought. Tomorrow would be an early day, and he needed to get some sleep. He knew sleep wouldn't come easy, though. The anticipation of another find would keep his mind working late into the night. Maybe he'd uncover a skull or mandible, maybe a rib or vertebra, maybe—just maybe—a set of antlers. *Hush,* he scolded himself. *Got to get to sleep.* His body wasn't what it used to be. He knew that, too. Emmett switched off his desk lamp, climbed into his cot, and slept the best he could.

✳ ✳ ✳ ✳

Bees. Bees were swarming him. Buzzing, buzzing all around. Emmett swatted at the air again and again before jerking violently awake.

It was 4:00 AM Thursday morning, and the alarm was going off. No bees, just the alarm driving him out of a deep, deep sleep. Rubbing his eyes, he forced himself to sit up, then to get up. He turned on a lantern and staggered over to the pitcher and water basin he always used to trim his beard and freshen up. *Empty, perfect.* He had forgotten to fill the pitcher the night before. He needed that splash of cold water to wake up his senses.

Emmett groped for a flashlight and found one. He moved through the dark to the tent opening, untied the bottom ties, ducked down, and groggily emerged on the other side. There he switched on the flashlight and stood up in the darkness outside. As he turned to make the trek to the camp's water tank, though, Emmett stopped short and instinctively took a step backward. His legs buckled, and a small, squeaky gasp escaped his throat.

Just feet before him, two large black bears stood on their hind legs swatting at a bundle of food dangling five feet in the air. Food bundles were usually hoisted about eight feet from the ground as a safety precaution to keep bears out of campsites and out of the food supply. But this bundle must have slipped and now these bears were using it as a piñata. One smacked it, then the other, until before Emmett's eyes, a hole ripped open and food tumbled to the ground. The bears quickly dropped back on all fours. Emmett watched in horror as their glowing eyes turned on him. One bear roared angrily, and Emmett's grip on the flashlight loosened. He screamed for help as the flashlight fell to the ground and went out.

* * * *

The bell attached to the lodge's screen door jingled as Gil poked her head into the lobby. "Phase one, done," she announced.

"Seriously?" Pike questioned, looking up from the game of bumper pool he and Griffy were playing. Griffy rested his cue stick against the table and gave Gil his full attention. He wanted to hear this.

"Yes, seriously. Did you think I was going to chicken out?"

"Yeah."

"How'd you do it?" Griffy asked.

"It was easy. I kayaked over around dinnertime last night and walked right into camp. You know, I *can* pass for a college student—as long as no one looks too closely. Besides, everyone was in the mess tent, anyway. No one even saw me." She arrogantly blew on her knuckles and rubbed them across her shirt.

Pike high-fived his sister. "All right, Gil."

Then he smiled shrewdly at Griffy, who gulped. It was his turn now.

A small setback, Emmett told himself. *Not to worry.* He stood at his washbasin and splashed cold water on his face. He paused, water dripping off his beard, and looked quizzically at the pitcher. He didn't remember ever refilling it after this morning's uproar, but he shrugged. *Oh, well. I must have. Old age*, he sighed. Emmett took a handkerchief and soaked it in the water. It was going to be a hot night. The cold snap ushered in by the storm had left, and now temperatures were rising again.

Emmett climbed into his cot, exhausted. The day had been a grueling one spent cleaning up and reinforcing food bundles. At the sound of his screams, the camp had sprung to life. It was instant chaos. Panicked students and bears ran everywhere. The bears—five in all—left a path of destruction before they were finally driven out of camp. No one knew how that one food bundle had slipped. The same knots and ropes were used on all the other bundles, and none of those had fallen. They'd also discovered traces of what appeared to be trails of food leading from the woods into camp. No one knew how that could have happened, either. *It was odd, very odd, but just a small setback.*

Sighing wearily, Emmett placed the wet handkerchief over his face and fell asleep.

He didn't need the alarm to wake him up Friday morning. Feverish, Emmett tossed and turned throughout the early morning hours. He was hot, flushed, and very sweaty. The cool handkerchief had long since dried up and fallen off of his face. He leaned over the cot's side and patted the tent floor until he found it, then he got up and went to the washbasin to soak the cloth again. As he dabbed his face soothingly with it, Emmett caught a look at himself in the mirror. *Strange*, he thought, leaning in for a closer look. The tent was dark, but still ... Emmett fumbled around for a lantern. He found one, switched it on, and quickly carried it over to the basin. For the second time in two days, a small, squeaky gasp escaped his throat.

His entire face was red and swollen. He looked disfigured as if he suffered from a strange disease. Some sort of large bumps or lesions covered his face. And suddenly—very suddenly—his entire face itched madly.

For the second time in two days, Emmett's panicked screams woke the entire camp.

* * * *

First thing in morning, Griffy ran down to the lodge's lobby. He couldn't wait to tell Pike. He flew through Uncle Dell's office and ran smack into his friend, who was coming around the register counter.

"Whoa," Pike called, grabbing Griffy by the shoulders. "Well?"

"I did it. I did it," he panted with excitement. "Phase two, done."

"Anyone see you?"

"Nope. Gil was right. College students really like to eat. No sign of Potts, either. I snuck right inside his tent." Griffy put his hand to his chest. His heart was thumping even louder than it had when he was sneaking around Big Crooked Lake the evening before. He took a deep breath and smiled proudly at Pike. "You're up."

Pike grinned and rubbed his hands together shrewdly. "Here comes phase three."

* * * *

Duck itch. How on earth did I get duck itch? And who knew it could be this bad? To wash, Emmett only ever used water from the camp's tank, and that water was boiled and purified. It made no sense. Nothing was making sense. First bears, now duck itch. Emmett shook his head in frustration. Setbacks. There were always setbacks. His whole life seemed to be one big setback.

Emmett poked at his face as he examined it in the mirror. He wasn't a vain man, but oh, Lordy he did look frightful. His eyes had swelled almost shut. Pink calamine lotion dotted the bumps on his puffy face. Although the lotion helped calm the itching, it cracked and flaked as it dried, making his face look even more dreadful.

I'm not going to let this stop me. This is not going to hold me back. Tomorrow is another day. With that motto in mind, Emmett swallowed two antihistamine tablets, put an ice pack to his face, and lay down to sleep his pain away.

When the alarm went off at 4:00 AM Saturday morning, Emmett was more than ready to get up and get moving. He was giddy with excitement. His face still ached and itched, but on the bright side, his eyes weren't nearly as swollen.

Emmett quietly snuck out of camp. The calamities of the past two mornings had left everyone sleep deprived, so no one was likely to wake up anytime soon. And that was good. Maybe the bear invasion and duck itch would actually work to his advantage, give him some needed time. *Things happen for a reason, right?* he assured himself.

Emmett made his way to the canoe he had left hidden near Big Crooked Creek. He pulled it into the water and pushed off as he climbed in. He seated himself and paddled through the creek's weed-clogged channels. It was dark and eerie. Emmett could barely see, but he didn't dare use a light. His excitement grew with each stroke. Finally, he was off to make another career-altering find. Emmett paddled faster, but then suddenly stopped as he felt something move across his ankle.

What was that?

Emmett shook his leg. He waited.

Nothing.

He began paddling again but then stopped. Something had pulled at the hairs on his leg. He shook the leg again and then slammed it hard into the bottom of the canoe. He waited.

Again, nothing.

He was about to put the paddle back in the water when the something crawled quickly up his leg. Emmett dropped the paddle and slapped at his leg over and over.

Missed it, missed it, missed it.

Legs—a lot of them—scurried under the man's thigh. Emmett jumped up on his knees and smacked the back of his thighs and calves. He turned frantically right and left, but he couldn't find it—whatever it was.

Then, he felt it. *Oh, no.* It had moved up his pants leg and up to his inner thigh.

Oh no!

Emmett quickly unbuckled his belt and drove his hand down his pants.

"*Ow, ow, ow!*" he cried out in pain as he pulled the six-inch-long crawdad from his shorts. Blood ran down his hand and forearm as the creature squeezed its large pincers tighter to his fingers. Fighting back the pain, Emmett shook his hand sharply.

The canoe rocked. But the crawdad held on. Emmett grabbed it by the tail and pulled, but still the crawdad held on. Emmett stood up, leaned over the side of the canoe, and readied to beat the creature against the boat's metal frame. However, as he swung his hand down, the canoe flipped over and plunged Emmett headfirst into the water.

It took Emmett almost three hours to pull his canoe out of the sludge that was Big Crooked Creek. He started back to camp, soaked and dripping with black goo. A scowl worse than any his students had seen that summer covered his face. His clothes were ripped and stained with blood. It was nearing 8:00 AM, so the camp would be wide awake and buzzing with activity. There was no way he could sneak back unnoticed, so Emmett lowered his head, deepened his scowl, and trudged onward.

As he reentered camp, Emmett stared straight ahead. He didn't look at anyone, didn't greet anyone. No one greeted him, either. In fact, they made every effort to get out of his way. When Emmett reached his tent, he grabbed the flap and, if a tent flap could slam, he slammed it shut behind him.

No one saw Emmett Potts for the rest of the day.

That evening, Emmett sat at his desk contemplating his next move. He couldn't wait any longer. It had been five days since his last find. The elk fossils had revitalized the camp, but the thrill of those finds would soon fade. His students would start talking, start asking questions, start looking a little closer at those bones. He needed more, much more. Emmett stroked his bandaged hand.

What to do? What to do?

He didn't have a choice, did he? It was do or die now. He'd get a fossil tonight no matter what stood in his way.

FOILED

Griffy's walkie-talkie squawked to life. He jumped out of bed at the sound, grabbed the gadget, and quickly pulled it to his face. It was Danny, not Pike just playing around again.

"Activity at the lagoon. Not bears. Over."

Griffy's stomach flipped. That meant Potts was there. He hadn't expected this. It was a gutsy move on Potts's part to go to the lagoon this early, just after 9:00 PM. The setting sun still glowed orange across the lake. It was a Saturday evening, and fishermen would still be out on the lake. Potts, Griffy thought, was either dumb or desperate.

He, Pike, and Gil had been taking turns keeping an eye on the lagoon for the past three days. Griffy was scheduled for tomorrow's early morning patrol, so he had gone to bed early. But as no one had seen any sign that Potts had returned, they were all beginning to wonder, especially Danny, if their tricks really had worked or if they actually had been wrong about Potts.

Griffy's hand trembled slightly as he held the walkie-talkie. He suddenly felt hot, and his throat tightened.

"Roger that," Pike's voice crackled over the airwaves.

Gil's followed: "En route."

Griffy swallowed hard and pushed the talk button. "Roger," he finally croaked out. He got dressed, grabbed his gear, and very quietly climbed down the loft's ladder.

His job now was to get the cart and drive it over to the swim bay unnoticed. *No problem*, he thought, surveying the Whispering Pines grounds. No one was out. *Good.*

Just as he pushed the gas pedal, a loud bark echoed through the still evening air. Griffy's whole body jumped at the sound. *Spinner.* He turned to find the dog seated in the back of the cart. "Shhh!" Griffy scolded. Spinner wagged his tail excitedly and barked again. "All right, all right. You can come if you stay quiet." Griffy motioned for the dog to lie down. He noticed Spinner's tattered cast and gently swatted the dog's nose. "And stop chewing on your cast."

Griffy pulled the cart to a stop near the swim bay and waited for Pike and Gil. They would be taking the cart down to Sleepy Eye. That section of Peninsula Road had finally been cleared—at least enough for the cart to get through. Griffy heard the faint hum of a motor and soon saw the lights of *The Lucky 13* coming around the bend. He exhaled deeply. *Here we go.*

About fifteen minutes later, Danny greeted them at the top of the Sleepy Eye driveway.

"I wasn't quick enough," he whispered. "Potts has been in there a while now. I've heard him moving around and talking to himself. Got to hurry. Come on."

Gil, Pike, and Griffy each quickly strapped on a cow horn and threw camouflage netting over their heads. Pike had taken the netting from his dad's hunting supplies. It covered each of them in small, greenish brown leaves. The cow horns came from Pike's own collection and served two purposes. First, a hard blow on one would scare any bear away. Second, a soft blow mimicked the call of a loon perfectly. It would be their signal, and Potts would never suspect it. Finally, the kids each grabbed a flashlight and followed Danny down the hill.

Through the leaves and netting, Griffy watched Pike and Gil separate and move into the woods. They looked like horror movie creatures—creepy, like mutant bush people, he thought. Their leaves rustled in the wind as they slowly became one with the forest and disappeared. When Griffy could no longer see their shadowy figures, he turned and headed for his own position at the mouth of the lagoon.

They had made it just in time. Potts was packing up. Griffy crept close to the lagoon's shore and crouched among the trunks of a small cluster of birch trees. He grabbed the end of the rope lying there and waited for the signal. His body tensed with anticipation. He absently rubbed the scar on his left arm as he watched Potts climb into his canoe. *Come on*, Griffy's mind cried impatiently. Potts picked up the canoe paddle. *Come on*. Potts began to propel the canoe forward with quick forceful strokes. *Come on!*

Then he heard it.

Ouooooooooo! A loon's call filled the night air. It was Gil's cow horn.

Griffy sprang to action. He pulled as hard as he could on the end of the rope. It grew taut instantly as Pike pulled on the other end. The rope they had hidden across the mouth of the lagoon popped up out of the water and hit Potts mid-stroke and mid-chest, causing the paddle to fly out of his hands as he jerked backward.

Clotheslined!

The canoe tipped over, dumping Potts and all his gear out. The three kids cheered and then quickly fell silent.

Potts slowly got to his feet and, standing still in the water, looked around suspiciously.

Griffy froze.

"Who's there?" Danny shouted angrily. He stepped out from behind a tree. "I know you're there, *Professor* Potts," Danny taunted from the bank. "Gotta watch those ropes. They'll get you every time."

Potts let out a roar. He ran through the shallow water and dove for Danny. Danny bobbed and weaved, but with only one punch, Potts knocked him flat.

Griffy gasped. He instantly ran to help Danny. Gil and Pike had the same response, and soon strange bush creatures surrounded the lagoon. Potts spun wildly around. "What?" Fear and confusion filled his voice. The three bushes moved closer.

"I'll get Danny," Gil shouted. "You get the fossils."

At her order, Griffy turned on his flashlight, changed direction, and ran into the lagoon. He searched the water near the canoe. Soon, Pike was at his side scouring the water, too.

"Got it," Pike announced excitedly as he pulled a satchel out of the water. "I saw him put— ugh!" Pike grunted as the upside-down canoe suddenly crashed into them.

Potts.

Griffy tried to steady himself but couldn't. He fell backward, and the canoe moved over him, trapping his legs. Pike didn't fall, but he dropped the satchel and his flashlight. He shoved the canoe back at Potts and away from Griffy, and Potts pushed back, causing the canoe to smack Griffy in the chest. He tried to scoot himself out from under it, but the camouflage netting kept him tangled. He watched helplessly as Potts and Pike wrestled each other over the canoe. He knew Pike was strong but didn't know how long he could last against Potts.

Then to Griffy's surprise, Potts fell forward, hit his head on the bottom of the canoe, and disappeared behind it. Pike gave the boat one final shove. Griffy rolled out of the way and quickly untangled himself from the camouflage netting.

"Didn't see that coming, did you?" Danny shouted.

Griffy grabbed the satchel and a flashlight from the shallow water as he got to his feet. Danny was standing in the lagoon pumping a hockey stick up and down in the air. Gil was right behind him.

"Blind man's bluff, old man," Danny yelled. "I wasn't down for the count. Not by a long shot."

Potts held his head as he slowly regained his footing. "You'll pay for that," he bellowed. But instead of diving for Danny, he lunged angrily at Pike and Griffy. Griffy's eyes widened and his stomach clenched as Potts knocked the unsuspecting Pike down and then headed straight for him.

"Give me that!" Potts demanded as he lurched forward.

Griffy did the only thing he could think of. He reached into the satchel and pulled out what was inside. It was a fossilized mandible. He threw the bone as hard as he could toward the shore and Sleepy Eye.

"No!" Potts yelled. He jumped up to intercept, but the bone just cleared his hands. As Griffy watched the mandible sail through night sky, he prayed he had thrown it hard enough and far enough.

But wait. What's that?

Griffy saw something in the sky, something flying through the air.

Is it a bird? A bat? Griffy waved his flashlight upward. *It's Spinner!*

The dog caught the bone in midair, better than any dog Griffy had ever seen playing Frisbee in Grant Park. "Run, Spinner, run!" he shouted.

And the dog did just that. He hit the ground running.

As Potts turned to chase Spinner, the three kids pounced. But just as they were about to ensnare him with Griffy's camouflage netting, the glare of a spotlight blinded them all. Everyone froze.

"What's going on here?" a voice demanded. Then the voice softened. "What on earth? Dr. Potts, are you all right?

Griffy tried to shield his eyes from the glaring light. *Does Potts have an accomplice?* He gulped. *We're in trouble now.*

Potts pushed away from the kids. "Yes, I am quite all right, thank you. I'm glad someone has finally arrived."

Just then Griffy got a good look at Potts for the first time that night. His hand flew to cover his gaping mouth. The sight must have startled Pike and Gil, too, for Griffy heard them gasp. Potts's face was a bumpy, lumpy mess. It also looked as if pieces of it were cracking and peeling off. His eyes were swollen to narrow slits. Gauze wrapped around one of his hands was bloodstained and unraveling.

Griffy flinched. *Did we do that?*

Pike snickered guiltily and whispered. "Guess our sabotage plans worked."

"You!" Potts turned on them, enraged. "It was you. All of you! Who—who *are* you?" he demanded.

"Never mind that," the voice behind the spotlight said.

"Never mind?" Potts shouted back, using his hand as a shield against the light. "These people have been interfering with important research."

"There's been no research," Danny countered. "There's been trespassing and theft."

"I've been doing scouting in the area. This lagoon could be my next dig site. I've been studying this area for months. I've ..."

"Save your breath, Dr. Potts," the spotlight-cloaked voice said sympathetically. "I saw everything."

"Did you?" Danny challenged. "And who are *you?* This is *my* property, and Potts here is trespassing."

The light lowered, and the figure moved closer. Griffy took a step back. "Jo!"

He had never been so happy to see the DNR, and he had never been so shocked to see Spinner trotting obediently beside Jo, the mandible firmly in his mouth, the cast on his hind leg gone.

"Yes, Griffy." Jo smiled reassuringly at him. "Pike. Gil." She nodded at each of them. "You can take the camouflage off now." They obeyed. "I've been watching this lagoon for the past three days. Got a tip from Dell that some suspicious activity might be going on. Seems he was right."

Surprise flooded Griffy's face. *Uncle Dell?* He beamed happily. Uncle Dell had been there for him all along. He hadn't abandoned or dismissed him at all. Uncle Dell had come through. *Wow.*

"I've told you," Potts started.

"And I said, save it," Jo ordered. "Sheriff's on his way. Gloria Nordman, too. You're finished, Potts."

THE SLEEPY EYE ELK

Griffy ran down the driveway at Sleepy Eye Rentals. He had just finished his chores at Whispering Pines and was eager to get to the lagoon. Uncle Dell had agreed to go easy on Pike and Griffy—work-wise, anyway—for the rest of the summer so the boys could spend more time at Sleepy Eye. Griffy stopped about halfway down the sloping drive and took in the scene below.

Archaeology students from the University of Wisconsin–Madison milled about taking notes and setting up equipment. A protective tent covered the lagoon area, which had been dammed and drained of water for the excavation. So far, a skull, a set of ribs, and the second antler had been uncovered. The radiocarbon tests had proven what Griffy had suspected all along. The elk dated to 8,000 BC, making it about ten thousand years old. The skeleton was the oldest anthropological find in state history and would be forever known as the Sleepy Eye Elk. Requests were pouring in to study the elk and the site.

Griffy smiled as he watched Danny emerge from the Sleepy Eye office, rope in hand. He and Gil carried between them a bucket filled with ice and pop. The two had set up a concession stand for all the tourists stopping by. Never one to miss a promotional opportunity, Chequamegon Lake Association president Andy Gibson had made sure word about the elk spread fast, and now Danny was organizing and charging for tours.

Griffy's smile spread wider. Danny would never be alone or abandoned again, that was for sure. He could afford to hire full-time help now. And as part of the excavation deal, the university and the Minong Natural History Museum agreed to rehab his property. Sleepy Eye Rentals was starting to look good, real good.

"Yo, Grif!"

Pike emerged from the woods near the lagoon, waving. A tourist group followed right behind him. Spinner followed, too, carrying in his mouth a replica of the first femur bone they'd found. "Come on. I can use your help," Pike called.

Pike really liked playing tour guide. And he was good at it, Griffy thought. Pike's interest and enthusiasm over the Sleepy Eye Elk had impressed Griffy—a lot. He studied almost every night trying to learn as much as he could about fossils and archaeology. It was rare now to see Pike without a book in his hands.

Griffy waved back and was about to run down to meet Pike when two cars pulled in behind him and parked in the gravel lot next to the Sleepy Eye office. Andy Gibson and Gloria Nordman, the Minong Natural History Museum's executive director, stepped out of one car. Griffy saw those two a lot these days.

"Griffy," Andy called, beckoning him. Griffy trotted toward the cars, but he stopped short. A woman had gotten out of the other car. Griffy did a double take.

"Mom?"

He couldn't believe it. His mother was here.

"Corbett!" she cried happily as she ran over to greet him with a big hug.

"It's Griffy," he corrected her. A little embarrassed, he glanced over his shoulder to see if Pike was watching. He wasn't.

"Right," his mom said. "Sorry." She smiled brightly at him. "Surprised?"

"Yeah. What are you doing here?" He was shocked, stunned even. His mother never took vacations or anything.

"Well, I convinced the *Sun-Times* that the Sleepy Eye Elk excavation would make a great series of stories, especially since one of Chicago's own was involved in its discovery." She tousled Griffy's hair. He grimaced slightly and pulled back, but inside he beamed proudly. "I also convinced them I was the best person to cover the story, since you are *my* son. We've even got a photographer. That's Jack." She pointed toward a guy whose head was now buried in the car's trunk. Jack waved his hand without looking up. "I'll be here the rest of the summer," she continued. "It's a big deal, you and this elk. We'll be putting the series out for the wire services and everything."

"That's way cool," Griffy gushed. He tugged on his mother's arm. Excited to show off for her, he said, "I'll give you the tour. But first, you've got to meet Pike."

Griffy's mind drifted as he and his mom walked down the hill arm in arm. Everything had worked out. The power was back on. Mossy Rock was blown up, and the road cleared. Potts's plan was foiled, and Danny was rightfully getting the rewards. And now, his mom was here to spend the rest of the summer with him. Not only was everything going his way, it was going everyone's way. Nothing could possibly go wrong now. It was all good.

"So what happened to Dr. Potts?" his mom asked, pulling Griffy from his thoughts.

"Oh, he's ruined, definitely ruined. He got a few choices. Retire or be fired. He retired. Community service or jail. He chose community service. He's doing time at the Wilderness Walk right now. Pike and I saw him." Griffy chuckled. "He gives talks about the animals every hour, on the hour."

His mom nodded and chuckled, too. Then she stopped walking. Griffy followed her gaze toward the lagoon. "Strange," she said.

"What do you mean?"

"An elk being found in the water. It's strange. Who would have ever thought to excavate the lake bottom? I wonder how the elk ended up there. You know, what his story was."

Griffy nodded. "Yeah, so do I."

"We'll probably never know that, huh?"

"Nope, never will," Griffy replied, but then he smiled knowingly. "Lost Land Lake holds a lot of mysteries."

"Grif!" Pike yelled impatiently. "Hurry it up."

Griffy grabbed his mom by the hand. "Come on." And together they ran down the hill toward Pike.

EPILOGUE: A PLOT

The SUV sped down County K toward Highway 27. The driver took a gulp of Diet Coke and glanced at the *Minong Ledger* lying on the passenger seat. She read the newspaper's front-page headline one more time: "Tourism booming at Lost Land Lake. Ancient elk lake's latest draw."

Lost Land Lake, she fumed. *It was always Lost Land Lake this, Lost Land Lake that. World Record Muskie. Ancient Elk. Blah, blah, blah.*

She was sick and tired of it. If it weren't for Andy Gibson and those darn kids—oh, and let's not forget that DNR ranger—her resort on Spider Lake would be booming. But now ... she shook her head in disgust. Now she couldn't fill her cabins. Now she was losing money. Now she couldn't pay her bills. Now she was facing foreclosure. And there was only one place to lay the blame.

Lost Land Lake.

She snatched the newspaper off the passenger seat, angrily wadded it up, and threw it out the car window.

Just ahead, she could see the sign. "Wilderness Walk. Open Daily, May thru September, 10:00 AM to 6:00 PM."

Poor Dr. Potts, she thought. She hated these goody-goody-type family attractions. Snotty-nosed kids everywhere. Crying kids. Messy kids. Loud, obnoxious kids. If she could ban kids from Empire Lodge, she would. She had already banned dogs. Kids were no better.

She turned the SUV into the Wilderness Walk lot and parked. It was closing time. She waited.

There.

The man exited the main building. *Poor, poor Dr. Potts.* A man of his intelligence, and standing reduced to entertaining children. It was downright appalling.

She backed the SUV out of its parking spot, slowly pulled up beside Emmett Potts, and leaned her head out the car window. "Excuse me, doctor. Can I buy you a cup of coffee?"

He waved her off and kept walking.

"We have some things to talk about, you and I. We have the same enemies, I believe."

That got his attention.

"We do?" he asked. He eyed her suspiciously, but nevertheless, she saw curiosity in his face.

"Yes, and I've got a proposition that I think will interest you." She smiled and nodded toward the passenger seat. "Hop in."

Emmett Potts obliged. As he pulled the passenger door shut, the SUV peeled out, leaving a trail of dust behind it.

AUTHOR'S NOTE

Ancient Elk Hunt: An Up North Adventure was inspired by the discovery of the Silver Beach Elk in Middle Eau Claire Lake near Barnes, Wisconsin. For more information, contact the Barnes Area Historical Association.

Be sure to check out *Muskie Attack* and *Snakehead Invasion*, the first and third books in the *Up North Adventure* series.

It's a quest of mammoth size: catching a seventy-pound beast stalking the waters of Lost Land Lake.
Are two young boys up to the challenge?

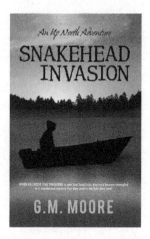

When an exotic fish threatens to ruin Lost Land Lake, two boys become entangled in a treacherous mystery.
Can they protect the lake they love?

www.facebook.com/upnorthadventure